The Love Formula

Michael David MacBride

DEDICATION

To all the romcom-makers and romcom-lovers out there.

ACKNOWLEDGMENTS

Thanks to Richard Curtis for answering my email about *Love Actually*. It was a simple thing, but often those simple things mean so much.

HELLO

Hello. That is both a chapter title and a greeting.

Did you ever notice that in books, the voice, or storyteller, is called a narrator, and in films, it's called a voiceover? We both perform a similar function, interjecting with asides and offering insight that would be otherwise awkward to include in conversation. You know, things like:

In 2009, Jenna McGuire, Michael Posada, and Kathy Armstrong developed a service called The Love Formula. It achieved one of the rarest things possible: no user complaints. The media took that to mean it had a "100% success rate," but the team winced whenever it was pitched that way. They were just glad they were helping people find happiness.

Of course, something like that could have been included in an interview, but you get the point. Sometimes that narrator or voiceover is the main character's internal monologue, and sometimes the voice belongs to someone you meet later in the story or film, like the child of the main character. I assure you, that is not the case in this instance. I am just the storyteller, but I'm also independent from the voice of the author. We are not one and the same.

Here's another short burst of information you'll need to know before we begin the story:

The three loved coffee and music and spent a fair amount of their time drinking coffee and talking about music before their lives were consumed with launching The Love Formula.

Some narrators disappear into the story and get out of the way, which is the way of movies without voiceovers or screen titles or any visible mark of the director. Some traditionalists call a voiceover in film "lazy" and then you end up with situations like *Blade Runner*, where the director's cut has a voiceover but the theatrical release doesn't. (The director's cut with Harrison Ford's voiceover is the superior cut.) When it's done well, the voiceover works well. For good examples, just see *The Big Lebowski, Trainspotting, Election, All About Eve, Apocalypse Now, Y Tu Mama Tambien, Kiss Kiss Bang Bang, Clueless, Adaptation*, etc. A narrator performs the same trick. Even a subtle narrator nudges the story along and paints one version of a story that could have been told in many different ways.

Other narrators are chattier. I immediately think of the narrator of *Don Quixote* or the voiceover in *Stranger Than Fiction*. In those instances, you find out who the narrator is, but in some books and films, the voice is almost another character without ever resolving who this voice is. It's just a nameless "other" that is separate from the author. If you were to pin down that author, he or she would likely be hard-pressed to identify where that voice came from. It was just the tone and style that made sense for the story to come forth.

I'm somewhere in between "invisible" and "chatty." I'm happy to get out of the way of the characters and let them do their thing, but there are times when I'll simply have to step in. For example, time jumps. Even if it's just to say, "three months later!" or "yada yada yada, now the friends found themselves at Tree Town Coffeeshop," those are essential transitions. If this were a screenplay, you'd have stage directions, like "Interior Coffee Shop", or maybe there'd be notes directly to the actors to help them get into character. But, since this isn't a screenplay, notes and asides and whatnot are for the benefit of the reader. At least, I hope you see them that way. They are meant to complement the story, not get in the way of or distract from it.

One of the neat things about a screenplay—again, which this isn't—is that they can simply state facts about characters. Whereas novels typically must find creative ways to describe characters. Maybe they stop to look in a mirror, which allows the author the opportunity to describe what the character looks like. Or maybe there's a straightforward description of a new character when they step into the scene. The trick is to make each character unique, but not to overdo it. Too much detail gets lost in translation. But if you can focus on one trait or unique characteristic that provides the reader an anchor, that works. Joe has a big nose that looks like cauliflower. Kimberly always wears a brooch her mother gave her. Something like that.

Michael is the twitchy, anxious one. Kathy is the steady, thoughtful one. And Jenna is some kind of blend of the two of them. They were all born in and around Ann Arbor and they met in college—don't worry, you'll get to know them better, these are just the broad strokes.

That quick overview is key to where the story begins. Which is Ann Arbor, Michigan, in 2010—the Love Formula has just passed its one-year anniversary and it's going strong. In fact, they've even secured enough money to produce some advertisements. Sure, I could have had one of the characters read a newspaper or walk the streets of the city and see a movie debuting in the theater that would help anchor it in time. Jenna could skip by the Michigan Theatre or go out of her way to walk by Michigan Stadium (even though Jenna and her friends didn't hang out on that side of town). I could have done something more subtle, and if you, dear reader, had cared enough to look up what Nickels Arcade was, then you'd know we were in Ann Arbor.

Call it lazy if you want, but I call it being direct and considerate of your time. Kurt Vonnegut, one of my favorite authors (and here the author and narrator agree), offered some advice to writers in his short story collection, *Bagombo Snuff Box*. Of the eight pieces of advice Vonnegut offers, there are two that I keep closest to my heart: don't waste the reader's time and give your readers as much information as possible as soon as possible. Which is what I always aspire to do.

The last piece of information you need, before I set you loose into this world, is that this novel has a soundtrack. A single Beatles song alone would prevent this from ever being an official soundtrack to a movie version—much less the four included—but in a book like this I can mention the songs and help set the mood. Just like a good movie soundtrack, there are some songs that appear during the course of the film, the ones that are actually featured in key scenes, and then there are others that fit with the tone and mode of the story but won't be included in the film's score. The same is true here. Some of these songs are mentioned directly and others complete the audio portrait of the book but aren't directly called out.

Here is that soundtrack, in a very particular order:

The Love Formula

A — Noise Reduction: × — EQ: High(CrO₂): 70µs

1. Musta Got Lost (live) – J. Geils
2. The Waiting – Tom Petty & HB
3. Norwegian Wood – Beatles
4. Just What I Needed – The Cars
5. And Your Bird Can Sing – Beatles
6. Take A Chance – ABBA
7. The Lovecats – The Cure
8. Too Much Time – Styx

B — Noise Reduction: × — EQ: High(CrO₂): 70µs

9. I'm Looking Through You – Beatles
10. It's the Love – Breeders
11. While My Guitar... – Beatles
12. I Believe in a thing Called Love – The Darkness
13. Too Late for Love – Def Leppard
14. Maybe I'm Amazed – Paul & Wings
15. Where Did Our Love Go? (Live) – J. Geils

ADVERTISEMENTS

"There's this one," Kathy says, and hits play.

A man (30) and a woman (30) sit at a table in a dingy bar. Loud music is playing. The woman is mouthing words to the man, but they are indistinguishable from the music. The man works his tongue across his teeth in an attempt to dislodge food. He spills his beer and the liquid races towards the woman. She sees it coming and tries to back away in horror. A female voice cuts through the music and says: "I am so tired of the same old dating scene. I need a way to find a better match."

"And this one."

A man (45) sits in front of his computer wearing only tight, formerly white underwear. His hair is greasy and uncombed and his belly hangs over the stretched elastic of his underwear. He scratches himself as he looks at his computer screen. The computer shows his recently uploaded profile picture. The photo is of the same man, but 20 years younger and fifty pounds lighter. A male voice asks: "Who am I kidding?"

"And this one."

An attractive woman (37) and a sharply dressed man (41) sit at a table in a fine restaurant. Wine glasses are half full and the plates display the remains of assorted shellfish. The woman checks her cellphone and picks her nose. A male voice says: "Is she bored? What's going through her head? Neither of us are getting any younger here."

"Annnd, one more," Kathy says, hitting place once more.

On the front stoop of an apartment, a woman (23) reaches in her purse for her keys. She searches around trying to find them. A woman (22) stands on step below, waiting. The first woman finds her keys, looks at the other woman, they lean in and kiss. In unison, two female voices say, "Finally, I think this is the one."

The one kiss blossoms into another couple kissing. Then another and another. Men kissing women. Women kissing women. Men kissing men. Different ages. Different ethnicities. The scenes duplicate slowly at first, and then gain speed, until the entire screen is full of couples kissing. The lighting in the scenes change, some lighter and some darker, until the words "The Love Formula" emerge.

Kathy reaches out and closes the laptop. She and her two friends, Jenna and Michael, are in Jenna's apartment. It's sparsely decorated but shows some amount of style and a few pieces of value. For example, the Miro is not a print. In addition to the painting, there is also a large whiteboard on another wall. There are various notes on the whiteboard from a previous conversation, and each friend holds a marker.

"Well," Kathy asks.

"I like it," says Jenna.

Both women turn to Michael, who is wedging his tooth under his thumbnail.

"I'm not chewing my nails," says Michael. "Just cleaning under there."

"You say that, as if that makes it any better," says Kathy.

"That's one hundred times worse. If you have something under your nails, there's a sink right over there."

All heads turn in the direction of Jenna's kitchen, which is mere feet from where Michael stands.

"Yeah," says Michael. "But there's something satisfying about getting it this way."

"Anyway," says Jenna. "The advertisement?" She tucks stray hairs behind her ears.

"It's…" Michael trails off. "Fine?"

"Boy, that's a ringing endorsement," says Kathy. "What's wrong with it?"

"Nothing," says Michael. "It really is fine. Uhm, perfectly competent. It does exactly what it needs to."

"'Perfectly competent'?" asks Kathy. "Seriously?" She adjusts her glasses which have slid down her nose.

"What! That's a compliment!" insists Michael. "Do you know how few things or people are perfectly competent?"

"Michael," says Jenna. "I'm sorry to break this to you, but perfectly competent is not a compliment in anyone's book. It's the equivalent of being told 'you'll do for the moment'."

"If you went out with someone, and they said you were perfectly competent in bed, you'd take that as a good thing?" asks Kathy.

Michael looks at his thumbnail again. "Well, I mean. Not every night can be fireworks and Sting-like tantric lovemaking. Some nights have to be competent, satisfactory, good, fine."

"Okay," says Kathy. "What would you do, with our ad, instead?"

"I just feel like those are all scenes we've seen before," says Michael. "In movies or real life or whatever."

"That is what she was going for," says Jenna. "Something that seemed familiar and that we've all seen before. To introduce this new product to change all that. You know, with real people? Or at least people who seem real?"

"Right, and I get that," says Michael. "But I feel like the ad should embody more of that difference. It's dramatically different and unique, so the ads should feel like that."

Kathy nods and shrugs her shoulders. "I can see that point. Do you have any recommendations?"

"Jenna has that interview with Thomas Sillinger," Michael says. "Maybe we wait and see how that goes, and use clips of the interview to sell The Love Formula?" He looks at his thumbnail, catches Kathy looking at him, and sits on his hand instead.

"Oh no," says Jenna. "It's already bad enough that I'm being called 'the face of the company,' I don't want to be in every advertisement we have out there."

"But you are, literally, the public face of the company," says Michael. "I mean, not that we voted on it or anything, but you gotta give the public what they want. Right?"

"Right," says Kathy. "And you know, Mikey and I are fine not showing our pretty faces." She smiles.

"What about you two?" asks Jenna. "This company isn't just me, and I'm afraid that interviews like the one tomorrow, are going to make it seem like I created this. All on my own. And then if I'm in the ads? Ugh."

"Definitely appreciate that," says Kathy. "But you did scribble the idea down on a bar napkin. I mean, it sounds cliché, but that part is true. That was all you."

"It wouldn't have gone from bar napkin to what it is today with you or Michael though," says Jenna.

"I also appreciate that," says Michael. "But we, I think," he looked at Kathy to confirm, "are okay with you being the public face."

Kathy nods.

"You're better at talking about the company," says Michael. "I get lost in details and tangents."

Kathy nods again and rolls her eyes.

"And you just have a better story," said Michael.

Jenna groans. "The story of the person who created a love-finding site but can't find love herself?"

"It is memorable and endearing," says Kathy. "And, like Michael said, you do seem comfortable in the public eye."

"Do you know how hard I have to work to pump myself up to do that?" asks Jenna. "Before I have an interview, I almost always have diarrhea."

"Gross," says Michael, scrunching up his face.

"Oh, like we all haven't had nervous diarrhea before an interview or a date or something," says Jenna.

"Uh," Kathy says, shaking her head.

"Yeah," says Michael. "Not me either."

"Weird, I just thought everyone did," says Jenna. "Anyway, it doesn't come easy to me. That's all I'm saying. Look, interviews aside, you say my story is a good thing, but I see it as a liability."

"Again, with that 100% match thing?" asks Kathy. "Just because you haven't 'found love' means you can't talk about love? And, for the record, I think most people would be happy with someone who is a ninety percent or eighty percent match, and you've had a few of those." Kathy removes her glasses and rubs the bridge of her nose.

"I know, one hundred percent. One hundred percent. One hundred percent! It has to be 100%!" says Michael.

"I just," Jenna starts and then stops. "What if my relationship fails, and I can't find a one hundred percent match, and I'm the public face of our company. What then? Then we're all ruined."

Michael laughs. "Look, the reality is relationships end. It happens to the best of us."

"I'm only looking for the one hundred percent, because the others aren't working," says Jenna. "If I could just find a hundred percent match, then there wouldn't be anything missing."

"The others aren't working because you sabotage them? Or because they're not actually a good match?" asks Kathy.

"I just want this thing to work," says Jenna.

"Me, too," says Michael. He scratches his head and runs a hand down the side of his face.

"Make that three of us. We need something you're comfortable with. We don't want to put you in an awkward situation, but with the press and the interview on Channel 56 coming up, they will have done a lot of the work for us," says Kathy.

"I'd like to take a second to pause here," Michael says. "Just to acknowledge something we really haven't talked about."

"What's that?" asks Kathy.

"That we have an actual company. I mean, it's really just the three of us," he laughs, "but we have an actual, real registered business. With real customers. And a budget for advertisements."

"Yeah," says Jenna. "It is pretty awesome."

"Granted, we might disagree about what those advertisements should look like," says Michael.

Kathy and Jenna groan.

"Yes, some of this would be easier if there were just two of us," Kathy says, winking at Michael.

Michael gasps in mock horror.

"What if we use interviews from our users?" asks Jenna. "Like, just real people talking about using the service?"

"I'd like to take this moment to point out that you are one of our users," says Michael.

Jenna frowns at him, and then writes, "user interviews"

on a white board hanging on the wall.

"I think user interviews are a great idea, but we need to give potential new users some of the information up front. Something about the verification process," says Kathy. She takes the dry-erase marker from Jenna and writes, "new user education" on the board.

"Right," says Michael. "They need to know up front that this is a different system. We don't want them getting to the page and turning away because they can't jump on board and just go."

"You think they'd jump ship because they had to stop at a pharmacy or government office to get a photo taken and verify some information?" asks Jenna. "I haven't seen that feedback from users."

Kathy and Michael both nod.

"Nothing says we can only have one kind of ad," says Michael. "We can have some customer spots, talking about successful matches. We can have some that are educational. You know: sign-up, get verified, take the test, set your parameters, find your match."

"The second kind will need some finessing," says Kathy. "Because it hardly sounds sexy or like it would have anything to do with love."

"Guess it does sound very transactional, doesn't it?" asks Michael.

"Right, but maybe we can combine these two?" says Jenna. "Customer satisfaction videos singing praises and telling potential new customers about how it works?"

Kathy writes "COMBO!" on the board.

"Combos!" says Michael. "I used to love those snacks. Do they still make them?"

Jenna ignores him and then writes, "montage of kisses" on the board and mocks wincing in pain. "Too cheesy?" she asks.

"Nah, I think it's sweet," says Kathy.

"You know what was cheesy?" asks Michael. "Combos! I think it's time to see if the party store has some. You gals with me?"

Kathy and Jenna both click the caps onto their markers and the three friends make for the door.

THE INTERVIEW

Jenna had always heard that television stations had a green room and was curious to see what one actually looked like, but instead of being shown to one, she was brought to the set and left to stand right behind the cameras. It's an interesting perspective, and she appreciates it because it give her a clear view of what was to come. There's s Thomas Sillinger, mid-fifties, a weathered newsman that she'd grown up watching her whole life. Next to him is Tina Frayer, younger, probably still in her thirties, who balanced Sillinger's dry take on the news. She's the new talent with a sense of humor, and Jenna likes that. The weatherman, Jim Dandy, is sipping coffee off to the side of his green screen. Yes, that is his real name. He was probably teased mercilessly at school, but he made the best of it now with lines like: "we have a Dandy of a weekend in store!" and "it's not great, but it's just Dandy!" And now, suddenly, Jenna is going to share a stage, or at least a screen, with them. Fortunately, she doesn't have too much time to overthink it, or she might have started to get overwhelmed.

She hears Thomas Sillinger queuing up their segment: "The answer to love comes in the form of a mathematical equation. Who would have thunk it? An interview with Jenna McGuire, the girl everyone wants to know, coming up after these messages."

Holy shit, this was for real.

An assistant ushers her onto the set, attaches a mic, adjusts her hair, and then she is just sitting there with Tina and Thomas.

"Good morning," Tina says. "This should be fun!"

"Thanks!" says Jenna. "I'm looking forward to it."

Sillinger smiles and scratches the side of his nose.

The producer announces, "thirty seconds." Jenna freezes and it is the longest thirty seconds of her life. Sillinger is saying something and then Tina takes a turn. Jenna's mind is racing, not quite putting together the actual words they're saying.

Then, something clicks and Sillinger's words make sense to her. "So, Jenna. Tell us a little about yourself."

"Well, I always wanted to be a writer. But, my verbal scores on the SAT, GRE, and all those other tests were always considerably lower than my math score."

"But you have an MFA, right? So you still pursued that dream," adds Tina.

"Right. I do. I did. You know, it's a rough market out there for writers. If you're not Stephen King, or Rawling, or whoever, it's tough to survive by craft alone." She scratches at her left wrist.

"True," says Thomas. "Well, let's move onto what America wants to know. How did the formula come about?"

"It started on a bar napkin, actually."

"Oh, that's funny," Tina says. "Tell us more."

And Jenna is struck by the fact that Tina genuinely

sounds interested. Either she's a very good actor, with years of practice in front of the camera, or she likes a good story, or maybe she's even a potential client. Jenna files this away for later because Kathy will want to know.

"My friends, Michael and Kathy, and I were all at a bar. We were talking about how difficult dating is. And how the Internet claims to have the solution. Yet, the divorce rate is pitiful." Jenna tries to look apologetic and adds, "sorry" to Sillinger. Suddenly sitting next to him, she realizes this piece of her sales pitch might hit a little close to home, as he just finalized his third divorce last month.

He smiles and shakes it off. Tina chuckles.

"We talked about how the Internet does have a leg up on the traditional bar scene because you get to know the person inside as opposed to just seeing a pretty face," says Jenna.

"You mean," says Tina. "Because on the internet, you have the ability to see more about the person than their looks? Without the kind of conversation that would happen at a bar? Over loud music and noise?"

"Hey, people meet at places other than bars and the internet," Sillinger says.

"True," Jenna says. "Like work, or museums, through friends, and of course there are other ways."

"I'm just saying," Tina adds, looking at Sillinger, "there are problems with some of the traditional settings where we meet. Is that fair?"

Sillinger nods and Tina turns to Jenna.

Jenna laughs. "Right. The three of us started talking about where relationships had fallen through before. Things we wished we had known before we got involved. You know," says Jenna.

"Right, again, I've been divorced three times. Sadly, there's a lot I wish I had known before getting involved," says Sillinger.

Jenna laughs. "Exactly! Divorces are expensive undertakings. But they're also hard on your soul. Think about it, each time you think you have a successful relationship, and it falls apart, you're less likely to open up to the next person." She's getting excited and realizes she's rocking a bit in her chair.

Sillinger nods. "That's a good point. We develop a thicker skin, so to speak."

"And thicker skin makes it more and more difficult to open up and have a healthy relationship," says Jenna.

"And yet," says Tina. "We learn so much from dating and relationships, don't we?"

"Oh, for sure," says Jenna. "So there's a balance. You want the experience without the hurt that leads to putting up barriers."

"Some barriers are essential though," says Thomas. "You wouldn't want to repeat the same mistakes again and again."

"Yes," says Jenna. "Good point. But you also have to be vulnerable enough to give the new person a chance without punishing them for the sins of previous relationships."

"I like that," says Tina. "Protective and vulnerable. A game of balancing."

"Honestly," says Jenna. "I was just trying to find something that would solve the dating dilemma for my myself and my friends. I don't mean to pretend that I would solve the world's problems or anything like that, just to be clear."

"Crystal clear," says Thomas.

"The problem with the web is that you never know if the person online is being sincere or not. There's no double-check."

"Say more about that," Sillinger says. "What do you mean by double-check?"

"Well, you hear all the time how police officers pretend to be twelve-year-old boys to catch pedophiles. I'm not saying they shouldn't, but if a police officer can effectively be an under-aged boy, then who's to say I can't be 50 pounds lighter, younger, and ten times cleverer than I actually am?"

Tina laughs. "Anyone who has used a dating app can attest to that happening more than once. One time—no, I better not."

Jenna debates about pushing, then decides to pause and see what happens.

"Let's just say," Tina says, taking the bait, "the person I met wasn't as advertised."

Jenna smiles and nods at Tina. "One of the innovations of The Love Formula is that we require all photographs to come from a third party. A pharmacy or photo lab or government office—like where they take passport photos—someone who can verify you are who you say you are, and that the photo is current. Some of these locations will actually take a photograph for you."

"A passport to love," says Tina.

"Oh! That's good! Can we use that?" asks Jenna.

Tina nods and smiles.

"No, seriously," says Jenna. "Can we use that? That's really good."

Tina nods and Jenna maintains eye contact, smiling.

Sillinger coughs and asks, "How does the rest of the process work?"

"When you look at another user's profile, The Love Formula tells you what percent you match with that particular user. You can set your range and limits, and have our system send you profiles of people that fit that desired range."

"But there are stipulations, about the kind of date you can have, right?" asks Tina.

"Yes," says Jenna. "We have recommendations, but there are a couple of absolute no-nos. Like, dates can't last longer than eight hours. There can only be one kiss. And a few other rules."

"Only one kiss?" asks Sillinger.

"A lot can be learned with a single kiss. Maybe you feel the spark, maybe you don't," says Jenna.

"But, if the connection is there, shouldn't people be able to continue, uhh, 'progressing' with the date?" asks Thomas.

"No, that's the biggest fault we found in our experiences, and now the experiences of many others. That people rush into something they quickly regret. Passion is important, but love takes time," says Jenna.

"But, don't some people like that kind of thing?" asks Sillinger.

Tina gives him a look that Thomas misses entirely.

"If you want lust, go with that. If you want love, you need to work within our stipulations. Just one kiss," says Jenna.

"I'm going to challenge you on that point a little," Tina says.

"Oh?" asks Jenna.

"Lust and love aren't mutually exclusive, are they?" Tina asks.

"No." Jenna shakes her head.

"But it sounded like you were saying you had to choose," says Tina. "The lust path, or the love path."

Sillinger's head bounces back and forth between the two of them as they volley back and forth.

"Right," Jenna says. "That came out wrong. Let me try

again. Can we fix it in post?"

Tina and Sillinger laugh.

"No, this is live," Tina says. "But we're just talking."

"Well," says Jenna. "I certainly can't speak for everyone, but I know when Kathy, Michael, and I got together and talked about where things went wrong, it was often when we led with the more," she pauses looking for the right word, "carnal instincts."

"Say more about that," Tina says.

"Those kinds of feelings can cloud emotions and judgment," says Jenna. "And to be as objective as possible."

"For good science?" says Sillinger.

Jenna nods. "Right, to be objective, we're trying to remove as many variables as possible, and make sure your assessment, of the date, of the person, of the kiss, is as clear-headed as possible. Is that fair?"

"That makes sense," says Tina. "Thank you for clarifying."

"Okay, I'm with you," says Sillinger, nodding slowly. "You get your one kiss and go home. Now what?"

Jenna smiles. "Then you both go home and rate the kiss. The computer adjusts your percentages accordingly, and then it's up to you if you want to go on another date."

"So, what is the formula exactly?" asks Tina.

"I'm not the math person, so I can't tell you precisely. Plus, it's proprietary. But, speaking about it generally, when Michael, Kathy, and I were talking, we scratched down ideas about attraction and chemistry," says Jenna. "There's a balance there, and I think we've found the perfect Love Formula."

"All from a bar napkin," says Tina. "Wow. I love it."

"I'm sorry that we're out of time, because I feel like I, and America, could learn more from you," says Sillinger.

"If you want more, like I do, visit the webpage appearing at the bottom of the screen. You can also link to it from our webpage Channel 56. Jenna, thank you so much."

"Thank you, Tina. Thank you, Thomas."

Tina and Thomas smile and wave to Jenna, she is ushered off set, they take her mic, and escort her out of the building. Just like that.

When the segment aired later that night, the three friends gather in Jenna's apartment and watch it. For Jenna, it's surreal seeing herself on the screen, much less the edited version of the experience that she remembers. Her brain tries to reconcile the actual memory with what she is seeing.

"That was great!" says Michael as soon as it's over.

"Great? They cut out half of what I said," Jenna groans.

"It's national prime-time TV. You can't buy exposure like that," Kathy adds.

It was true. The network had cut out a sizeable portion of Jenna's interview. They chopped out the part about how the site required registered users to have pictures taken at places that would also confirm their identification information. They also required users to update their images every six months. Yes, a lot could happen in six months, but that way it inconvenienced users as little as possible. They also cut out the rather flirtatious chat between Mr. Sillinger and Jenna. She wondered if they would air that, and, until he reminded her that he was divorced multiple times, she was vaguely interested. But it might have just been being that close to someone who amounted to a celebrity in her book.

The most disturbing thing that they cut was the discussion about accuracy. This was very important to Jenna, and her friends. They had yet to have an unsatisfied customer. Granted, the site had only been up and running for three months. But, it had also been "beta tested" on their mutual friends for six months prior to its launch. No other sites, the group thought, could boast 100% success rate. And yet Channel 56 had cut that.

Perhaps because they were afraid of receiving angry letters if something went wrong. Perhaps because they were pinched for time. But wouldn't 100% success rate be something that would catch the viewers' eyes or ears? Jenna, Michael, and Kathy all thought so. Only Jenna didn't seem upset by this exclusion. She had hoped they would focus more on the humanistic elements of the system. How it was really personal, and all the painstaking doublechecks they put in the system to attempt to keep it honest.

She sighs.

"I'm glad they left the part in where you mentioned our names!" Kathy says, excitedly.

"Yes!" adds Michael. "We were on TV!"

"Good, I'm glad that you both focus on the important stuff," Jenna laughs. "Of course, they had to keep that part in. The people always want to know your humble roots."

"Yes, we are self-made men and women. That's attractive," says Kathy.

TREE TOWN COFFEE

Welcome to Tree Town Coffee Shop. Once upon a time, this building consisted of office space to rent with tiny apartments on the top floor and a recording studio in the basement. Well, actually, the recording studio—called Tree Town Studios—was in the second sub-basement. That studio was made popular in the nineties by a ska band called SKAborough Fair—Jenna's parents were fans—but with the dissolution of that band, the studio similarly dissolved. The exterior of the building consists of brick and glass. It's a beautiful space designed around a massive oak tree that grows up through the floors. The first basement is where its roots live, and each of the other floors has been designed around where the tree grows. There are spiral stairs to the right of the entrance, and a glass elevator that will take patrons to any of the three floors. So, calling it a "coffee shop" undermines its size and scope a bit.

The logistics of having a living tree and keeping bugs out of the coffee shop are worth considering. Just how would that work? In a movie, we'd rely on this as being so visually interesting that the viewer wouldn't have time to contemplate these concerns. In a book, there's more time to question the plausibility and of course, now I've called attention to it. Oops. The good news is: this is actually a thing! In fact, some architects build using living trees as support structures for buildings. There's a combination of mesh netting and other barriers put up to prevent unwanted insects from entering, but it's not perfect. So, yes, there are bugs inside occasionally, but not any more frequently than the insects that get in through the open door as customers come and go.

When Jenna walks in, she walks across the hardwood floors and to the counter, where the owner, Conrad (54) stands. Conrad is wearing a Tree Town apron over his Black Flag t-shirt, blue jeans, and sandals. His forearms are covered in tattoos from 80s punk bands (most notably: Black Flag and Bad Religion). His hair is disheveled, unkempt, and yet oddly stylish. Jenna runs her hand across the wooden countertop, which is rough-cut and looks like part of a tree trunk.

"Whoa, this is a change," says Jenna.

Conrad looks up and raises an eyebrow.

"Where's Grover? What's the boss doing running the register?" Jenna asks.

"Good morning to you too," says Conrad. "What can I get you?"

"Avoiding the question?"

Conrad shrugs. "I guess that's what I get for dating women half my age." He sighs. "Let's just say, you'll probably see more of me. Hopefully that's not a bad thing?"

"Not at all. So, Mr. Ink, I think I see a new one on your finger?"

"Yes," Conrad says. "Any guesses?"

Jenna looks at the very simple tattoo that runs the length of the inside of Conrad's left index finger. It looks like a mustache.

"Not really," Jenna says. "It doesn't look like any punk band logo I've ever seen, nor any grass roots movement, nor any anti-government message. So, either I'm out of the loop, which is distinctly possible, or it doesn't fit with the rest of your tats."

"Oh! An observant one. And yes," says Conrad. "You're right. This is whimsical. This is light! This is funny! This is…"

"I appreciate the compliments, if they were meant as such," says Jenna. "But I've been coming here since you opened and you've only ever had like three people work here. So, if I hadn't noticed your tattoos, I would have been painfully ignorant of my surroundings."

Conrad holds the finger to his lip and displays his mustache proudly. "A mustache!"

Jenna snorts and laughs. "Wow, I'm not sure what to say. A mustache? What happened to Mr. Serious? Mr. Saving-the-World? Mr. Grumpypants?"

"I think I'm done being angry. I've been angry for a long time. I'm ready for something new."

"Well, you know what they say. It takes more muscles to frown than—"

Conrad interrupts. "That's actually not true. But I appreciate the sentiment. Do you know why I got my first tattoo?"

"Because you loved your momma?"

Conrad laughs.

Another customer approaches the counter. Conrad nods to the newcomer, pours a mug full of coffee, and hands it to the customer. The customer wanders upstairs to find a table. No words are exchanged.

"No," Conrad says. "And it wasn't some girl I fell in love with. Once upon a time, I lived on a farm. I hated it as a kid, but as I got older."

"Wait. You? A farmer?" Jenna scratches her head and looks dubious.

"Why?" Conrad mimes using a pitchfork, followed by holding a piece of straw in his mouth. "That's so hard to believe?"

Jenna laughs and says, "Just trying to picture you in overalls. Wait," she closes her eyes tightly and then opens them again. "Okay, I think I got it."

Conrad shakes his head.

"Right, whatever. Dad was a farmer. I was supposed to inherit that farm and whatever, but I didn't want anything to do with it. Big business was making it hard on him. They were always selling him new equipment and tools to make his job easier, but of course, those things were expensive and so we were always broke. I hated that. When he died, we didn't have enough money to pay off the mortgages or even pay for a proper funeral."

"I'm so sorry," says Jenna; she leans on the counter.

"Rather than being a farmer, I became a lobbyist."

"You? Holy shit," says Jenna. "I thought you were Mr. Antiestablishment?"

Conrad ignores her and continues. "I thought I could help support farmers like my dad, by working for the American Farm Bureau Federation, one of the oldest lobbyist groups. I did what I could to fight for farmers' rights. The problem was, I was constantly getting crapped on. We were making deals and legislation was pending and dead in committee and I felt like I was selling my soul. Flying corporate jets, eating at fancy restaurants, you know. Meanwhile, where were the farmers? They weren't any better off than before. I started getting tattoos as a way of coping. First, I got these."

Conrad brings his hands forward and turns them over

to reveal UPC symbols.

"I felt like I was part of the machine," says Conrad. "So, I got the UPCs of the most commercial things I could think of. Any guesses?"

"A McDonald's hamburger?" asks Jenna.

"Good guess, but no. The right is a Barbie and the left is a GI Joe."

Jenna laughs.

"I thought you'd like that. Anyway, somewhere between the tattoos and punk music, I found my sense of balance. Eventually, I quit the corporate gig, opened Tree Town, and have been growing into this building ever since."

"Like the tree?" asks Jenna.

Conrad shrugs. "Never thought about it, but yeah. Like the tree." He holds up the finger to his lip again.

Jenna laughs. "Wow, that's quite the story. I had no idea you were such a softie."

"Don't let the word get out. It will ruin my rep." Conrad's eyes wrinkle up as he smiles.

"And the record studio?"

Conrad pours coffee into a mug when Jenna isn't looking.

"Yep," says Conrad. "I bought the sub-basement space and opened Tree Town Records first. That's where it all started. As I could afford more, I bought more and more space. When I got tired of recording, I turned over a new leaf with a coffee shop." He pauses. "Speaking of coffee, what will it be?"

"Oh, and here we are, right back to business," Jenna says. "Yes, a dark roast."

Conrad smiles and hands her the mug. "Kathy's up on two. Tell her to holler down if she needs a refill. I'll run it right up."

"Thank you," says Jenna. "Will do."

Jenna climbs the stairs, sees Kathy, and joins her at the table.

"Hey, did you see Conrad's new ink?"

"No," says Kathy. "Anything exciting?"

"Ask him to see it next time you're down there. It's funny," says Jenna. "You know, he's kind of sweet."

Kathy raises her eyebrow. "Old Sourpuss? That guy hits on everyone who walks through the door. Even me. If he's being sweet, it means he wants some."

"He's just," Jenna searches for the right word. "Amorous."

"Horny's more like it," says Kathy. "He kept hitting on me and wouldn't take the hint, so I outright told him I'm a lesbian. He just winked at me." Kathy shakes her head. "I will say though, his attention to detail is incredible."

"What do you mean?" Jenna asks, lifting her mug.

"Well, this mug for instance," Kathy holds up her mug. At first glance, it's identical to the one Jenna is using.

Jenna shrugs.

"Clearly you lack the observation powers of Connie," Kathy says, and then asks, "What do I do with my mug?"

Jenna looks embarrassed that she doesn't know.

"Ugh," Kathy sighs. "I rub the side of the mug and feel its imperfections."

Jenna rubs her mug with her thumb but doesn't notice anything.

"Yours is nice and smooth," Kathy says. She turns her mug to Jenna. "But mine," she demonstrates, "has this little bubble. Maybe it formed in the firing process, who knows. I mentioned it to Conrad once, and he's remembered it ever since."

"Wow," Jenna says. "That's really kind of sweet. Are you sure you don't want to have his babies?"

Kathy laughs. "Eww." She shakes her head to clear the image. "Anyway, we have more important things to discuss. You'd better be down for this!"

Jenna looks down at her chair. "I'm pretty sure I couldn't be any more sitting down if I tried. I am literally in a chair, sitting next to you. And you're also sitting."

Kathy ignores her and presses on. "Guess what?"

"Chicken butt?"

"Be serious! Come on!"

"You're in a good mood this morning and obviously more awake than I am?"

"Yes, and yes. But something else!"

"No clue, sorry."

Kathy sighs. "Okay. Get ready. Here it is. We got—" She looks around, sees no one on this floor, and whispers something.

"What?" asks Jenna. "I can't hear you."

Kathy whispers again, but it's completely inaudible.

"What?"

"Put these on," Kathy says, handing Jenna a set of headphones. She turns the laptop towards Jenna and says, "Just watch, it speaks for itself."

George Clooney sits casually on a stool in a plain gray room. He's dressed sharply in a suit, and a black tie hangs loosely around his neck. The room is painted a soft charcoal gray and is devoid of anything other than George Clooney and the stool upon which he sits.

"You know how hard it is to find love on the open market?" George asks the camera. "Well, now imagine you're famous. It's great. Believe me, but not when it comes to finding love. I've done alright over the years, but fame has its disadvantages, too. Being who I am, sadly, seems to bring out the worst in women. You have to train yourself to look through the deception and see the glimmer of who the person really is… and that takes work, and sadly it often leads to disappointment. I know you know what I'm talking about. So, what's the solution? I know I have a reputation as a prankster, but I don't mess around with love. I'm tired of being Time Magazine's most eligible bachelor. I need something to help me filter out opportunists and help me find companionship. A true partner. The Love Formula takes a lot of the guess work out of dating. I've been trying to do this for years, and The Love Formula just makes it that much easier. I found my match there, you should give it a try, too."

The video ends and Kathy says, "nice, eh?"

"Wow," says Jenna. "Wow. So, how exactly did we land Clooney?"

"He's kind of the poster child for the rich guy who dates waitresses," says Kathy. "Right?"

"I'm pretty sure he's dated his fair share of models and actresses, and maybe even been married?"

"Sure, he's no saint. Whatever. Anyway, he called us. Not his agent. Not his people, but George-fucking-Clooney called."

"Us? I don't remember hearing anything about it."

"Well, he called me, I nearly threw up when he said who it was."

"That's a strange reaction," says Jenna, trying not to laugh at her friend.

"I know," Kathy says. "I never really cared about celebrity, but somehow his voice just broke me. It was so obviously him, I never even stopped to consider it might have been a prank call."

"That would have been my first thought," says Jenna.

"Yeah," says Kathy. "You're the skeptic of the group for sure."

"Hey!"

"It's a good thing," says Kathy. "Someone has to keep Mikey and me grounded. Anyway, I thought it would be a nice surprise." Kathy shrugs. "So, uh, surprise?"

"Absolutely," says Jenna. "I just hope we have some ads that feature 'normal' people. I don't want to end up being the dating service for the stars."

"For sure, we have plenty of those." Kathy gestures to her laptop where there are twenty video files. "Each of these are ads with normal people. Our one hundred percent matches. Success stories. You know, those ones you're always obsessing about?"

"First, I love it. I love the look. I love that you just went and did it. I would have second-guessed it, and probably fucking freaked out if he had called me. Most of all, I love that I'm not in any of these." Jenna laughs and then takes a deep breath. "And as far as the one hundred percent matches: I don't obsess about them, I'm just happy to see the formula find true love for someone."

"Whatever, you totally obsess about these. I think it might be because you haven't found yours yet?"

"Maybe."

"What's your highest percentage so far?"

"Before or after the kiss?"

"Both," says Kathy. As she waits for Jenna to answer, Kathy opens another folder on the computer. "You'll notice, in these new commercials, we've gone with a simple background to really focus on the people. It was inspired by George's shoot."

"You're on a first-name basis now?" asks Jenna.

"It is his name, right?" Kathy asks. "Since I wasn't going to ask him to reshoot his, I figured it was easier to mimic that look with the others. Turns out, it's pretty cheap to do locally, so don't stress about the budget."

Kathy double-clicks another file on her laptop, but

mutes the volume. The commercial plays.

A woman sitting on the same stool, in the same charcoal gray room.

Jenna watches the video, but circles back to Kathy's earlier question. "I had a ninety-two percent once, but after the kiss it dropped to a seventy-two. Another one was eighty initially, and went as high as eighty-eight after the kiss."

"What happened to him?"

Jenna shrugs.

"Not a hundred, so not good enough for you?" Kathy asks. "You know, there are plenty of people that are happy out there with less than one hundred percent matches. Hell, there are even people in arranged marriages that end up happy with one another."

"I just don't see the point in settling," says Jenna. "If the perfect guy is still out there."

"Right, and how many dates have you been on now?"

"A woman never reveals her secrets."

Kathy double-clicks on another file. The next commercial plays.

A man sitting on the same stool, in the same charcoal gray room.

"Last I knew," Kathy says. "You were nearing a hundred."

Jenna sighs. "Pretty close."

"Slut!" says Kathy and laughs.

"Hey, you know the rules! I'm just kissing them," says Jenna. "How else am I supposed to know?"

"Hey, I'm just kidding," says Kathy. "Here, take a look at this one."

They turn to the laptop and Kathy unmutes the volume.

A man sits on the same stool in the same charcoal gray

room and speaks to the camera.

"If you need help finding a mate, there are plenty of webpages out there. There's always the bar scene, or the grocery store scene. You know, picking up guys near the rutabaga? Trust me, it works. But, you never really know who this person is. Is he putting on an act? Is he straight and just doing the groceries for his wife or girlfriend? Oh boy, I can't tell you the number of times… wow… how embarrassing. Most of the dating sites out there forget about their gay clientele. The Love Formula is different, it works for you if you're gay, or straight, or bi, or whatever. That's where I met Jeff, and we've been happily dating for three months now. He's my one hundred percent and the love of my life. Is your one hundred percent waiting for you? Check out The Love Formula and find out."

"I think that's my favorite," says Jenna.

"Yeah, mine too. I do think the gays are underrepresented out there in the dating-site world."

"Well," says Jenna, smiling at Kathy," It helps that we have one on our team. Has Michael seen these yet?"

Kathy's pocket buzzes and she answers her cell phone. Then realizes she hadn't answered Jenna's question and nods to her.

"Hello?"

"Hey, what's up?"

"Uh, you called me?" says Kathy. She laughs and then turns to Jenna, "It's Michael."

Jenna scoots her chair closer to Kathy and Kathy shares the phone with her.

"Is it safe to assume you have the other third of our group there?" Michael asks.

"Remember that deal we made with the devil?" Kathy says. "At least two of our members must always be joined at the hip?"

"Yes it is, no secrets here," says Jenna.

"Morning!" Michael says. "Okay, so I'm starring at four shirts, trying to decide which to wear."

"Awww, our little boy is all grown up and caring about his appearance," says Jenna.

Michael snorts. "I've always cared about how I look. It's carefully curated."

"Yes, you have a uniform of sorts," says Jenna.

"So, let me guess," says Kathy. "The shirts you're considering are all patternless button-ups?"

"Hey! They're different colors," says Michael.

Kathy cups her hands around her mouth and booms, "Boring."

"Are you getting ready, already?" asks Jenna.

"No?" Michael holds up a dark blue shirt and considers it. "Why do you even ask? Of course, I'm stressing and overthinking this. It's a big date. I landed a ninety-seven percent today. Have you decided where you're going with your Ms. Ninety-two?"

Kathy laughs. "We're going to start with dinner. Food's always good. Anyway, Jenna loved the commercials. Particularly the one with Stephen."

"Stephen?" asks Michael.

Kathy rolls her eyes. "You know, Stephen. The guy who addresses how most dating sites miss the LGBT community?"

"Oh, right," says Michael. "Jenna, I'm glad you liked them. I think they came out looking pretty sharp. At first, I wasn't sure about the plain background, but I think it forces the viewer to focus on the person. Look, I just called to say hey and to confirm we are getting together at Tree Town tomorrow morning, right?"

"Of course," says Kathy.

"We'll talk then," says Jenna. "All about your date! Have

fun!"

"See you," says Kathy.

Michael hangs up.

"I swear you could mark the hours of the day by that guy's neuroses," says Jenna. "I mean, I love him and all. But he's totally a bundle of nerves."

"I know," says Kathy. "He means well. I guess I should probably get ready too, eh? See you tomorrow."

Jenna smiles. "Tomorrow it is. Good luck, Kath."

"Are you going to get ready, too?" asks Kathy.

"I'm basically ready now," says Jenna. "I'm meeting David just across the street here."

"Alright, well, have fun!" Kathy shuts the laptop and walks down the stairs.

This is Jenna's favorite floor of Tree Town. Both of the upper floors have old, worn, but comfortable couches and chairs, but the second floor in particular has great lighting that pours in through the windows. It also helps that floor-to-ceiling bookshelves are packed with books. When she needs time to herself, she heads up to the third floor, because it's less frequently occupied. Though it's not an official policy, the third floor is typically a quiet place. But the second floor is where the group usually meets because the three of them are loud and have a hard time not talking to one another when they're together.

With her friends getting ready for their dates, Jenna finishes her mug of coffee and sits staring out the window, enjoying the view of the University of Michigan diag.

WHAT'S A DIAG?

Not "a diag," but rather "The Diag." Okay, so what's The Diag? I don't know if other cities have diags, but in this particular case, The Diag is a chunk of green space in the heart of Ann Arbor. It's called a "diag" because several sidewalks crisscross the space diagonally shortening the distance to walk from one end to the other. Clever, eh? But it's really more than that. So, bear with me for a short history lesson. I promise to make it interesting.

First of all, while the University of Michigan is associated with Ann Arbor, it actually originated in Detroit. What? I know. You've been lied to all these years. The university began life as Catholepistemiad in 1817. That's a full twenty years before Michigan even became a state. A few years later, people were making fun of the "academy of universal learning" because of its goofy name, and the board decided to rename it the University of Michigan in 1821. Sorry, Judge Augustus Woodward.

Who's that? Oh, he's the guy who came up with the name Catholepistemiad, and he's an interesting guy in his own right. Several people describe him as the prototype for Ichabod Crane in "The Legend of Sleepy Hollow." You know, skinny, tall, gangly, stooped, big nose, bachelor, loner who slept in his office. Because he was buds with Thomas Jefferson, he was appointed the First Justice of this new territory called Michigan. Woodward, after whom there is a major road in Detroit named, helped rebuild the city. Despite his slovenly reputation, he embraced the underground railroad and was instrumental in ensuring that fugitive slaves were allowed to remain free in the new territory and not returned to the south. Woodward had to flee Michigan during the War of 1812 but was able to return in 1813 to help rebuild after the evacuation of the British. Anyway, his buddy Jefferson and he collaborated on ideas and both the Catholepistemiad and the University of Virginia shared those basic foundational themes. Oh, and he was a Freemason.

Anyway, in 1821, it was officially the University of Michigan.

In 1837, the state of Michigan, because it was indeed a state now, decided to move the university to this fledgling town called Ann Arbor. The idea was Detroit was big enough on its own merits, but Ann Arbor needed a boost. Moving the university there would help bring people to this part of the state and businesses would be established and boom and all that. You have to remember, these days Ann Arbor is a short car ride from Detroit, but back in the day, forty-five miles (give or take) was a day's journey.

The state set aside forty acres for the university. This is what's now called Central Campus. The university has blossomed and grown out from there, but this is the core. This is the heart. And the heart of the heart is this square plot of green space, originally called the Diagonal Green, but now simply abbreviated The Diag. The Diag is bordered by State Street, North University, South University, and Church Street, though East University used to be the eastern border before it was truncated at South University and converted from road to sidewalk, essentially extending The Diag another 336 feet to Church.

This is the space where students gather to protest, this is where Hash Bash is held, this is where students lounge between classes and play frisbee or hacky-sack or read a book in the shade of a tree, or wander the art museum, or where you might hear a group of students playing Led Zeppelin covers on homemade instruments asking for tuna fish instead of tips. It's the sacred space. The libraries are here, where you can get lost playing hide and seek in the stacks—though the librarians discourage that. When JFK, Jr. visited the campus, his speech was given at the Michigan Union, which technically isn't part of The Diag, but students spilled over across State Street into The Diag proper in hopes of catching a glimpse of him.

The center of The Diag features a brass block M. Legends abound about the M and what happens if you step on it. So much so, that even non-believers go out of their way to avoid the M. Just in case.

Thus concludes the history of The Diag. Consider yourself informed, and now you're almost ready to get to the three dates the friends went on.

ARBOR BOWL

Sorry, I really did mean to move onto the next story but realized there's a little history to get out of the way before we do that. Though not quite the "landmark" of Ann Arbor that The Diag is, Colonial Lanes was a staple of Ann Arbor, too. Well, at least since 1962. It was tucked away on South Industrial, so it wasn't downtown necessarily, but it was the place to go if you wanted to bowl. Otherwise, you could head closer to Ypsilanti for the Ypsi-Arbor Bowl, but Colonial was closer to downtown and had better food. Though it had been updated here and there, Colonial Lanes looked like a '60s bowling alley. Depending on the decade, that was either cool or not, or retro or dated.

When they were trying to figure out where to go, Charlie and Michael both blurted out, "bowling?" And then laughed. Michael hadn't been able to win over Kathy or Jenna to bowling, even though he kept trying to convince them that bowling was an ideal activity for a first date. It was sport enough to be a competition, but with low stakes. You could participate while having a conversation. If you got hungry, there was food. If you wanted a drink, there was a bar. There was noise enough to provide a background to avoid awkward silences and it was public, while also allowing for the intimacy of your lane.

That's it. A much shorter history and I probably could have included it as an aside, but then I fear it would have slowed down that chapter and detracted from the date. So, I guess I'm leaving it here. Thanks for your patience. Now, really and truly, without further delay, the three dates.

THE THREE DATES

Jenna stands at the southwestern corner of The Diag, near a concrete kiosk that is covered from top to bottom in flyers, advertisements, and promotional material about upcoming concerts, political rallies, and the like. She divides her time between eying the materials, checking the time on her watch, and looking for her date. Students bustle to and fro. Some skateboard, others rollerblade, a few bike, but most walk. Some listen to MP3 players and bob their heads or sing out loud, some are deep in thought, some talk to one another, and a few talk to themselves. She feels invisible and loves the power it grants her to eavesdrop and people-watch. No one seems to recognize her or care that she was on television recently. Here, she's just another person on The Diag.

Across town, Michael walks in the front doors of the Arbor Bowl. It takes him a couple of seconds for his eyes to adjust to the relative darkness and then he begins scanning the people for his date. He walks to the counter to pay and swap out his shoes. As he's removing his shoe, he sees his date, Charlie (26), smiles, and waves her over.

In between the two locations, Kathy walks into Ray's

Red Hots, a small restaurant that specializes in "red hots." Most people would refer to these as hotdogs, but the owner of Ray's Red Hots and anyone else who knows better, would take offense. As Kathy walks in, she immediately recognizes Louise (40) from her photo, already sitting in a booth, and walks over to her.

"Wow, you look nice," Kathy says.

"Thanks," says Louise. "So do you. And might I compliment you on your fine choice of cuisine."

"Well, you know, these aren't just hotdogs. These are red hots."

"I know," Louise says. "It might have sounded like a joke, but I was being entirely sincere. I love this place."

"No kidding! I used to come here all the time. It's funny our paths never crossed before."

"Maybe they did, and we just didn't know it? Sometimes it's all about timing and being primed for the moment." Louise smiles. "Shall we?" She gestures to the counter.

"Absolutely." Kathy gets up and offers her hand to Louise. She accepts, and they both walk to the counter to order.

Meanwhile, at the bowling alley, Michael attempts some light humor.

"You know what they say about a guy who wears big shoes, don't you?" he asks.

"Oh dear," says Charlie. "That he has big feet?"

"Probably, that sounds about right. I only have a size nine though, so I never bothered to learn the rest of the joke."

Charlie laughs.

"Shall we, uh, go grab some balls?"

Charlie groans. "Is this how the whole night is going to go? Jokes about balls and penis size?"

"I swear, I didn't pick bowling for the ball jokes, but I just can't help myself."

"Well, that's good. Tone it down a few notches, and we should be alright."

Jenna checks her watch again and becomes engrossed in watching the secondhand move. It's a little herky-jerky, but she enjoys watching the circuit it makes around the watch face. David (31) taps her on the shoulder and jerks her from her daydream.

"Jenna, right?" David asks. "Sorry I'm late."

His touch and voice startle her and it takes a moment for her heart to slow and for her to respond.

"Yes," she says. "Jesus, you scared the crap out of me."

"You were rather absorbed in something," David says. "I couldn't tell what and wasn't sure how best to approach." He laughs as he says, "Clearly, I chose poorly and scared you anyway. Sorry about that."

"That's alright. I was just watching time pass. Literally. Quite mesmerizing."

"It is. I know what you mean," David says. "Shall we walk?"

"What exactly is the plan for tonight?"

"The art museum for a start. You game?"

"Of course," Jenna says. "I love the museum. It's one of my favorite places in the city. Or did you know that about me already?"

"Oh? If it said something about in your profile, I didn't notice that," David says. "It just so happens to be one of my favorite places in Ann Arbor as well. And I find that someone's taste in art reveals a lot about them. So, good guess? Happy accident?"

They step inside and wander from collection to collection, stopping occasionally. David stops in front of a painting.

"For some reason, this one never fails to grab me. It's just amazing."

"Miro's *Dancer*. It's a great piece. Movement, bold colors, it's really everything I love about Miro."

"Art major?" David asks.

"Once upon a time," says Jenna. "What about you? I have to admit, I didn't read your profile as closely as I should have. What do you do again?"

"I'm a Chinese archeologist," David says.

"Wow, well that would explain all your knowledge of the Asian collections," Jenna says. "Wait, are you messing with me?"

David laughs.

"Uh, huh, I see," says Jenna. "Are you going to tell me what you really do?"

"No. Do your homework next time. I'm shocked you didn't memorize my profile and study up on all my interests. Isn't that what people do?"

"Did you?

"No," says David. "I'm only giving you a hard time. I prefer to get to know people the old fashion way."

"How's that?"

"Through conversation and observation?"

"So, you're more of an anthropologist then?"

David laughs.

"Wait," Jenna says. "You do look familiar. Do I know you somehow?"

"Maybe from the picture in my profile?" David asks. "I have to be honest, before you asked me, I was about to ask you the same question. You look familiar, outside of the profile picture, but I can't quite place it."

"It's possible we've just crossed paths," Jenna says, shrugging. "We both live and work in the city."

"True," says David. "Or maybe we just look familiar?"

Jenna smirks. "Are you saying we look so common to one another that we're unremarkable?"

David laughs.

"No," David says, "I'm suggesting more like we fit the mold of the sense of beauty we've each developed over the years, starting with what our role models for happy relationships look like and all the media we've ingested over the year to determine what 'beauty' means to us."

"That's kind of deep for a first date, don't you think?" she asks. "But I see what you mean. Now that you mention it, you do look a bit like a mashup of my parents and some musicians that might have hung as posters in my bedroom as a teen."

David nods and smiles. "I'll accept that."

Michael's ball spins wildly into the gutter. He stands watching it in disbelief and then slowly turns around to face Charlie. She is laughing at him. He walks slowly to his place next to her and collapses into the seat.

"So, you're really not very good at bowling, are you?"

"Usually I at least break a hundred," Michael says. "I think you're intimidating me. You know, with your good looks and all."

"Uh-huh," says Charlie. "Should we get you some bumpers for the gutters?"

"Very funny. Let me rest my wrist."

"You'd think it would be stronger," Charlie says. "You know, with all that practice with balls and all."

"Oof!" says Michael. "Anyway… let's talk about something other than balls. Here's a good one: describe yourself in three words."

"Three words: concise, amused, and warm."

"Whoa, whoa, whoa! You did that entirely too fast. Was

that a rehearsed answer? Had someone asked that before?"

"No."

"No?"

"See also: concise."

Michael nods then and starts to laugh. "I see."

"Your turn."

"No, that was my question for you. You need to come up with your own. No cheating."

"What? What kind of weird date-Nazi are you? Three words. Describe yourself. Now."

"Right now?" Michael says, clearly stalling. "Amused? Uhm… amusing? And… uhm… intimidated?"

They both laugh.

"Ready to move on?" Michael asks. "I don't know that my wrist will ever be ready enough to overcome your scores of," Michael checks the score sheets and then continues, "225, 237, and 215. Oof. Maybe we could hit Jerusalem Garden for some falafels?"

Two red baskets lined with wax paper sit on the table in front of Kathy and Louise. Used napkins are bunched up on the table as well, Kathy slurps the last dregs of her soda through a straw.

"You know," Louise says. "If you want some more, soda isn't that expensive. I could probably spring for a refill."

"That's alright. I'm just enjoying the last little bit and thinking."

"About what? Penny for your thoughts?" asks Louise.

"Oh, just my enjoyment of beef franks with odd toppings. I mean," says Kathy. "Who would have thought to combine Russian dressing, Swiss cheese, and sauerkraut on a beef frank?"

"Apparently the owners of Ray's?"

"Good answer," says Kathy. "Good answer."

"Anything else on your mind? Hot dogs aside, that is?"

"Just that it's funny, I feel like I've known you before. We can talk and banter. Give each other shit. It feels very comfortable. And yet new?"

Louise nods. "Glad to hear it. I feel the same way and was worried it might be too soon to say something like that. Usually, there's all that awkwardness and posing and then months, or years of trying to cut through the bullshit to find out who this person you're with really is. Somehow, I feel like we've short-cutted the whole system."

"Does that mean we're cheating?" asks Kathy.

"Maybe? But why waste time with all that garbage, if we can just cut to the good stuff."

Kathy smiles.

David and Jenna continue to walk slowly through the museum.

"Okay, so are you seriously never going to tell me what you do?" asks David.

"Never. I'll never talk."

"Then it's not important."

"Really? Just like that? You didn't try very hard, wouldn't make a very good interrogator."

"Just. Like. That," says David. "And besides, this is a date, not an interrogation."

They walk in silence for a few seconds. Jenna grabs David's hands and spins him in front of her. They look each other in the eye.

"Okay, I give," says Jenna. "I'm a sociologist. Of sorts."

"Of sorts? What does that mean?"

"Well, I study the interactions of people. Relationships. Dating. Marriage. You know."

"Am I a test subject?"

"Maybe."

David considers this. "Part of the control group?"

Jenna shrugs.

"I'm mortified. I don't remember signing up for this study."

"Well, aren't all dates really just a series of tests? You and I meet, I know little about you. You know little about me. We talk, we interact. We gather data, test hypotheses. Gather more data. Based on your reactions to the things I disclose, I choose to reveal more information or change directions. If you say the right things, I may want to see you again. If you say the really right things, we might end up in the same room in the morning."

"That sounds pretty clinical," says David. "But, out of curiosity, just what are those really right things, exactly? For my data set."

"Stop changing the subject," says Jenna. "What do you do for a living?"

"I work at a museum," David says finally. "In fact," he whispers. "Just like you, I'm working right now. Keeping an eye on the artwork, making sure no kids attempt to stick gum to the priceless Miro or knock over a Beasley sculpture."

"What?" Jenna is shocked. "You're working right now? That's not fair." She punches David in the arm.

"Sorry, that was a joke. I do in fact work at a museum. This museum. But today is one of my off days. I work with special collections. They come in; I help set them up. I write little blurbs about the art and artist and make them look pretty for the customers."

"Customers? Art museums have customers?"

"Sorry, patrons."

"I see," says Jenna. "So, this is the exit. What do we do next?"

"I think that's a wrap."

"A wrap? Really?"

"Really. All I had planned was a stroll through the museum. Some conversation. A chance to get to know you." David pauses. "And, if I remember now this site works, we need to have a kiss."

"Do you want to grab something to eat?"

David looks down at his shoes. "No, not really."

"Alrighty then."

Michael and Charlie are sitting at a picnic table outside Jerusalem Garden. Michael has eaten all his food, but Charlie is still working on her falafel.

"Hey," Michael says.

Charlie acknowledges him by raising her eyebrows as she chews.

"I just want to, I don't know, say I'm sorry?"

Now Charlie's face scrunches up in question.

"I just mean, I can come on a little strong. If Kathy were here, she's one of my friends, she'd repeat 'a little' with a strong dose of sarcasm," Michael laughs. "I just, oh, I don't know. I guess I'm anxious? I've never really talked about it, but dates are hard on me. I want to be myself, so people know what they're getting, but in the process, I end up being a hyper-version of myself." He pauses. "Which probably a bit much for most people and I just hope I didn't scare you away."

Charlie finishes her bite, smiles, and reaches out to Michael with a finger. He is clearly uncertain but remains still. Charlie removes a piece of parsley from between his teeth.

"There, got it."

"Oh shit," Michael says. "How long has that been there? All night?" He uses the side of his finger attempting to brush away parsley that isn't there.

Charlie laughs and then softens into a smile.

"We only just got here a bit ago, it certainly hasn't been here all night," Charlie says, then adds, dating's hard for everyone."

"You make it look pretty effortless," Michael says.

"Thank you," Charlie says. "Let me assure you, it's a carefully maintained façade. But I appreciate it nonetheless."

Michael laughs.

"So, how'd I do?" he asks.

"You do come on pretty strong," Charlie says. "At times, I felt a bit like we were in a *Friends* episode."

Michael doesn't get the reference.

"You know? Joke, joke, joke?" Charlie clarifies.

"Sorry, really didn't watch that show," he says.

"We might have to rectify that," Charlie says. "Which is all to say, I'm still interested. After all, vulnerability is sexy."

"Oh yeah?" Michael asks, perking up.

"Very."

Charlie leans in toward Michael and they kiss.

At Ray's Red Hots on South University, Louise leans across the table and kisses Kathy.

At the museum, Jenna leans into David and they kiss.

David pulls away from the kiss, smiles, and then walks back into the museum. Jenna walks down State Street towards her apartment, considering the events of the night.

JERUSALEM GARDEN

Had David taken Jenna up on the offer to grab something to eat, Jenna would have suggested Jerusalem Garden. And then, they might have unintentionally ended up creating a double date with Michael and Charlie. However, David said "no" to food before Jenna even had a chance to mention the restaurant as a possibility. He didn't know it, but Jerusalem Garden was Jenna's very favorite restaurant. How would he know? He didn't ask and she didn't offer, she'd never mentioned it to anyone who would have recorded it and it wasn't indicated on her profile. But Jerusalem Garden was a bit of a test for her with dates. If they didn't like the food or setting, it was a deal-breaker for her. At least, that's what she said. There were exceptions, like Rowan, but we'll get to him later. But before we entirely leave Rowan for a later chapter, let's just say, it's in part because of Rowan that Jenna has hard and fast rules that she tries to adhere to.

Okay, now Jerusalem Garden.

The restaurant owners initially settled in Detroit in 1962, before eventually relocating to Ann Arbor. Yes, that's right, just like the University of Michigan this restaurant has its roots in the much-maligned city of

Detroit. The owners opened the little restaurant (350 square feet) with $10,000 in 1987 on Fifth Street, right next to the Ann Arbor District Library's parking lot. The father died six years later, in 1993, and the restaurant passed onto his three children. One of them focuses on the falafel, another on managing the restaurant, and the third on hummus. In 2008, they expanded the business to almost three times the size (1,100 square feet) and began doing the majority of their business with dine-in, instead of carry-out.

So, what does Jenna love about this place?

One year, during Art Fair, when all the other restaurants were full, her mom brought Jenna here. They stepped inside the tiny atrium and stood near the counter. They didn't know what to order. A smiling man, the father, offered to help.

"What would you recommend?" Jenna's mother asked.

"You're here for the Fair?" the man asked.

Jenna's mother shrugged and looked embarrassed. "We are."

Being embarrassed about attending the Art Fair when you live in the city is not uncommon. Particularly when you are visiting a local restaurant where the workers are stressed, harried, and insanely busy.

"Well, then I recommend a falafel with hummus," the man said. He smiled at the blank looks from Jenna and her mother. "It's like a, uh, wrap? You can carry easy and it's delicious."

"Two falafels with hummus then," Jenna's mother said.

The meal affected the women in different ways. Jenna's mother decided, "I'm really not a fan of Middle Eastern food. Too much sesame," and never went back.

But Jenna fell in love with the food that day and that love extended to the restaurant and its employees. She'd notice a new decoration, or hear a new piece of the family story, or meet a new employee who shared a favorite item from the menu that Jenna had never noticed before. She learned the man who served them on that day, was Ribhi Ramlawi, and how he smiled at everyone, made them all feel welcome. She learned he brought the recipes from the "old world" and his children use those same recipes today.

One week she'd try baba ghanough and decide, "this is my favorite." When someone would ask what baba ghanough was, she'd say, "it's hummus with eggplant instead of chickpeas," which really didn't win it any fans. The next week, she'd claim the mjaddara was her favorite. Then grape leaves. Then fattoush salad. Then tabbouli. With each successive visit, she had a harder and harder time limiting her favorites to match her appetite.

So, when David passed on getting food with her, it wasn't just a disappointment because the date was cut short, it was also that he had passed on one of her very favorite places in the city.

ACT II

If you've already read the 1978 book *Screenplay* by Syd Field, then you know, Act II is where the stakes are raised for the hero (or heroes) to achieve his or her or their goal. The conflict increases and challenges amount.

If you haven't, then succinctly: most films (or stories for that matter) follow a three-act structure:

Act I: an introduction to the characters and the problem they're facing. By the end of Act I, you should know who the main characters are and what they want. Who are we dealing with? What's the premise? And where we are at in the situation?

Act II: Mr. Field calls this the "confrontation," but it's generally the "meat" of the story. This is where you spend most of your time. The goal is clear and known, but challenges present themselves to keep the character (or characters) from achieving it.

Act III: resolves the story. In short, does the character achieve his or her or their goal?

Oh, there are nuances, like there's inciting incident, rising action, midpoint, pre-climax, climax, denouement, and so on.

All this to say, we've reached Act II of our story. If this were a film, you'd be about twenty minutes in. Screenplay is so ubiquitous that even people who haven't read it, follow the structure and timing. And I should point out, Field didn't invent this method. He simply tapped into films that came before him, observed, and fine-tuned the approach.

So, welcome to Act II. You know a bit about the characters, where the story takes place, and what they want. Let's see if they successfully achieve their goals and make it to the denouement. But truly, if you've seen even one romantic comedy, you have a good sense of how this will end.

SO, HOW'D IT GO?

Conrad is happily cleaning the countertop with a rag and humming a song to himself. It's indistinguishable but appears upbeat. He looks up when he hears the chimes over the door as Jenna enters.

"Morning," he says.

"Morning."

"What's shaking? What's doing? What's going on? What can I get for you?"

Jenna looks at him, puzzled. "What's with the new chipper attitude?"

"Get used to it. This is the new me. I've turned over a new leaf. Yoga, better diet, and I had a tattoo removed yesterday."

"Does that hurt?"

"No, you just need to work on your flexibility, then the poses are a breeze."

Jenna laughs.

"Of course, it hurts," says Conrad. "Twice as bad as when I got them the first time around. But it's kind of like a weight was removed from my shoulders. An albatross if you will."

"Oh, a literary reference and it's only nine a.m.? Isn't it a bit early for Coleridge?"

"Okay, grumpypants."

"Hey, that's our name for you!" says Jenna.

"Not anymore," Conrad says. "Let me look in my crystal ball and see if I can figure out what's wrong. Shh! This requires absolute quiet and concentration." He mimes looking into a crystal ball on the counter and waves his hands around dramatically. "Yes! Yes, it's coming clearer. I see… oh! Of course! You hit your hundredth date last night! And still haven't found true love."

Jenna sneers at him and asks, "You talk to Grover yet?"

"That's just mean," says Conrad. "You're just trying to bring me down."

"Well," says Jenna. "There are all kinds of other fish in the sea, right? Isn't that the advice they give when you have a breakup?"

"Do you know how hard it is to find someone with a unique name like that?"

"Grover?" Jenna asks. "That's seriously not her name, is it? I just always assumed it was like a nickname or something."

"Hey, a former president was named Grover," says Conrad. "Well, middle name. But it's what he went by."

"What was his first name?" asks Jenna.

"Stephen."

"Oh, didn't know that," says Jenna. She mentally catalogs this information for later use. "Still, what's so important about a unique name?"

"It doesn't come with the extra baggage that a common name does," says Conrad. "You know, a Jennifer or a Christopher, there are so many of them out there. You're bound to have known at least one, and so when you meet someone with the same name, it takes a while to overcome your preconceived conceptions of who a Christopher or a Jennifer are."

"Huh, I honestly never gave that any thought," says Jenna. "But it's interesting to consider."

"It's also rare for someone to have a name that really, really, really suits them," says Conrad. "You know, like when you see someone named Tina and they so are not a Tina?"

Jenna raises an eyebrow.

"Or before a guy introduces himself, you know his name is Brian because it just fits?" Conrad asks.

Jenna shrugs.

Conrad sighs. "Oh well. Yes, Grover was her real name. And it suited her. And it was original. And"—he sighs again—"I loved her."

Jenna feigns surprise and alarm. "Did she die?"

"You mock my pain," says Conrad.

"Life is pain," finishes Jenna. "I'm just saying, there's a lot of past tense there."

Conrad nods. "Anyway, love. Yes, still love."

"Where is your dream girl, then?" asks Jenna. "And why haven't you fixed whatever you fucked up?"

"It's not that easy," says Conrad. "As I'm sure you know. She quit. Which, honestly is probably a good career decision."

"Not a lot of money in the barista business, unless you own the place," says Jenna and smiles at him.

"Enough about me, what do you want to drink today? Ms. Hundred Dates," he says. "You know, as if you have the whole love game figured out."

Jenna either doesn't hear or chooses to ignore him. She appears distracted as she looks at the board of drink specials.

Conrad mixes a drink while she tries to choose. He tries

to break her from her trance by adopting the accent of the Impressive Clergyman in *The Princess Bride* (1987). "Wuv, twoo wuv…" It doesn't work.

"Huh?" Jenna appears to finally catch up. "Oh god, is it that transparent? Kathy's been talking to you?"

"Well, they are also my customers. So, yes, I do talk to them. But in this case, it was Michael. He and Kathy were in a fine mood this morning. Something's going right for them. Sorry it's not for you."

"Good," says Jenna. "Happy for them. I don't know why I look at this board, I always get the same thing. Wake-up juice, please?"

Conrad turns to face her, handing her the drink he's been mixing.

"My specialty. You're a creature of habit, kid. Enjoy."

The irony of a coffee shop selling "wake-up juice" was always intended as a joke, but no one's ever commented on it to Conrad. It's essentially an espresso shot in a light roast coffee with a sprinkle of raw sugar and cinnamon.

Jenna nods, smiles, grabs her mug, and heads up the steps. Conrad smiles after her. She finds her friends sitting on an emerald, green couch. She joins them and, between sips of their various drinks, they chat.

Kathy opens with, "So, how did it go? From the looks of things, not so well. Or are you just that tired?"

"It was fine," says Jenna. "We had a great time. He seemed like a nice guy. We talked, but he cut the date short. I felt like I could have spent hours with him. I thought he felt the same, but…"

"Maybe had something else to do?" Michael says. "I mean, how long did you spend together? What did you do?"

"And how was the kiss?" asks Kathy.

"Let's see. In reverse order. The kiss was good. No, great. I rated it a ten."

"Ooh! Nice! Is that the first ten?" asks Kathy.

"Yes. It was a nice kiss. What's that Adam Sandler and Drew Barrymore movie? You know, that line about 'church tongue'? That's what it was like. No swallowing the face. Not a peck. Left me wanting more."

Michael offers, "*The Wedding Singer*. Enough with the mushy stuff. My questions now."

Jenna scrunched up her face in thought. "We spent, probably two hours together? Wandering the art museum."

"Art museum?" Michael interjects. "Well, I guess that suits you. Two hours though?"

"Do you think that's too long, or too short?" asks Kathy.

"I mean, personally, two hours in a museum feels like an eternity," says Michael. "But I recognize I'm not the art lover that you are. But, two hours for a date feels… abbreviated, at least to me."

"Does it?" Jenna asks.

"It's not about duration, but about quality of time," says Kathy. She turns directly to Jenna and says, "Don't listen to him."

"Hey!" says Michael. "She needs someone to temper the good angel on her shoulder, doesn't she?"

Kathy shakes her head and then asks, "Did you go anywhere afterward?"

"No. That's what I'm saying. He cut it short. I asked about getting something to eat, and he just said no. Enough about me though, tell me about your dates."

"It's possible he just wasn't hungry," says Michael.

"Or tired," says Kathy.

"Or not hungry and tired," says Michael.

"Or maybe he was bored and didn't want to spend any

more time with me," says Jenna. "Or didn't have the same reaction to the date and kiss that I did?"

"Hard to say," says Kathy. "My date was great. I feel bad gloating when you're obviously unsettled. But it really was like the perfect date. We hit it off immediately."

"Same here," says Michael. "I finally found a woman who can give shit as well as she can take it. Plus, she rocks at bowling."

Jenna laughs. "Being good at bowling is a plus, always comes in handy. Is that one of your requirements for dating? Excellent skills at bowling?"

"No, but it's certainly a perk," says Michael. "You know, a woman who knows how to handle balls."

Kathy and Jenna groan.

"Really?" Jenna says.

"Sorry, just couldn't resist. Anyway, so what are your percentages now that you've entered the kiss?" Michael asks.

Kathy shrugs. "I don't know. I honestly haven't looked. I'm not sure it matters. I know how I feel, and as long as Louise wants to go on another date, I don't care what the numbers say."

"That's the thing," says Jenna, ignoring Kathy, "not only did David cut the date short, but he hasn't rated the kiss yet. So I don't know."

"It's possible, just possible, that he was busy last night and didn't get around to it," says Michael.

"Why are you defending him?" asks Jenna. "You don't even know him."

"I know, and I love you, but you jump to assuming the worst in these situations," says Michael. "Back me up Kath."

Kathy nods. "I know you're frustrated, but there are other possibilities that might have prevented him from extending the date or entering the kiss data."

Jenna scoffs. "Extending the date? He cut it short. I wanted more. I wanted to go to Jerusalem Garden."

"Oh, the true test of any relationship," Michael says. "Had you gone, you might have run into us."

"You went?" Jenna asks.

"I know it's your favorite place and all, but you don't have exclusive rights to it," Michael says, laughing.

Jenna nods. "Sorry, just feeling a bit burned that I thought things were going so well, and then it's over."

"Not *over*, over," says Kathy. "You don't know. At least, not without asking."

Jenna mulls that over before saying, "But I see what you mean."

"I mean," says Michael, "he might want to really think about this. Maybe he takes this whole kiss rating thing super seriously."

"Then again," says Kathy, "maybe he's one of those people whose computer desktop is cluttered with documents and lack any sense of organization." She shudders.

"Oh Jesus, I hope not," says Michael. "That's a deal breaker. We should totally put that in the screener questionnaire."

Jenna frowns and takes a sip of her drink.

"Okay, so now the real question," says Michael. "Are you going to cheat to see how he scored the kiss, or how he did on Kathy's double-check quiz?"

Kathy shakes her head. "No. You can't. If you want to use the system, you have to have faith in how it works. Otherwise, go with your cut and how you feel. But no, you can't use your admin access to see all the data."

"I have to admit to being tempted," says Jenna. "Aside from the date being cut short, it really was pretty great. And why shouldn't I know? Isn't a relationship about trust and not keeping things from one another?"

"Would you share your answers with him?" asks Kathy. "Relationships are first and foremost about honesty. If you want to get together and share your answers with one another, sure, why not. But it's not fair that you'd have a glimpse into something that's meant to be private without his consent."

Michael nods. "Agreed."

"I have a bit of news too," says Kathy.

"Oh?" asks Jenna. "The last time you had news, it was George Clooney."

"What now?" asks Michael.

"Well, you know that hot dog place I went to with Louise?" Kathy asks.

"I thought they were red hots?" asks Michael.

"They are," says Kathy. "But I was afraid if I said that, you'd ask about it. I never know what you pay attention to and what you don't. Can I go ahead with the story?"

Michael and Jenna nod.

"There's a new owner, Ray. He needs help building a webpage and creating some buzz," says Kathy. "So he has some contests to encourage people."

"And since you're with The Love Formula," says Jenna. "He thought you'd be a great get?"

"What?" Kathy's puzzled. "No." She shakes her head. "No. But Louise and I really had a good time there, and we started talking about entering the contest."

"Which one?" asks Michael.

"Oh, the History of Ray for his 'about us' page," says Kathy.

"Shouldn't that be written by, like, Ray?" asks Jenna.

"He's a quirky guy and the restaurant has a funny vibe," says Kathy. "The contest asks for one small paragraph. I figured; we could do that. Then Louise starts telling me this funny story about how she was introduced to the restaurant. It was making me laugh so hard. I told her that she should enter the contest, but she was all, oh no no I'm not a writer. She said I should write it, and I said it's not my story to tell. So, we're collaborating!"

"To write the History of Ray?" asks Jenna.

"Yes!" says Kathy. "It's been a while since I've written anything funny."

"When do we get to read it?" asks Michael.

"It's almost done," says Kathy. "I'll send it over as soon as we're both happy with it."

"Well, that is unexpected," says Jenna. "And cute and awesome," she adds, smiling.

Michael raises his mug, "to the historian in the group!"

Kathy laughs and raises her mug. "Thank you. But, more importantly, to a night of, mostly—" she nods at Jenna, "—successful dates?"

Michael touches his mug to Kathy's, and eventually Jenna raises hers. They clink mugs. Kathy and Michael stand, both give Jenna a hug, and then head down the stairs.

Jenna remains at the table lost in her thoughts. She mumbles, "One hundred dates… one hundred dates…" Each of her one hundred dates flashes through her mind. Initially the images flip by slowly. The first kiss is at normal speed. Jenna leans in and kisses the guy from her first date using The Love Formula. The kiss ends; they smile and look at one another. But after the first, the images flip by faster and faster, until last night's kiss with David. The image of her kiss with David lingers in her mind.

She mutters to herself as she finishes her coffee, shakes her head, puts on a hopeful smile, and walks down the stairs.

THREE BRIEF FLASHBACKS

Now that we're squarely into Act II and you're left wondering how David's kiss scores, it's time to stretch out that anticipation a bit with a couple of flashbacks. Typically, these would happen with one of the characters in the middle of a conversation, suddenly zoning out, the screen going soft around the edges, and a new scene replaces the previous one. Or, maybe there's an abrupt cut and you don't realize you're in a flashback until the character awakens, or is startled out of his or her reverie.

Is it cliché and trite?

Yes.

Then why do we still do it?

Well, in part, because viewers expect it. In fact, they kind of demand it at times. They want to know the backstory, but only the relevant parts, and only after they've gotten to know the characters enough to care about their backstories. So, you jump into the middle of the story and begin there, and then flashback only as absolutely necessary.

Because it's so common, you don't want to overdo it though. However, some films can pull off the neat trick of rearranging the plot so you move forward and back without it feeling overdone or like a cheat. Think Christopher Nolan's *Memento* (2000), Michel Gondry's *Eternal Sunshine of the Spotless Mind* (2004), or Quentin Tarantino's *Pulp Fiction* (1994). It's impossible to imagine those films working any other way without manipulating and scrambling the timeline.

If you're a fan of flashbacks, then you're in luck! What follows are three flashbacks, one each for Kathy, Michael, and Jenna.

If you're not a fan of flashbacks, then you're in luck! You can skip this chapter. The rest of the book works without this knowledge. Hopefully, the flashbacks provide great depth of character and an insight into motivations and formative moments, but if that's not your jam, then skip ahead.

Kathy's flashback:

Kathy (16), Mom (40), and Dad (39) are all sitting around the dining room table. It's a large, heavy wooden table that has clearly served many generations of Armstrongs. They've finished eating and are talking about their days.

"Robby and I broke up," Kathy says.

"Oh?" Dad asks, raising an eyebrow.

"Oh dad, you never even liked him," says Kathy.

"That doesn't mean I can't be sympathetic, does it?" he asks.

"I'm sorry, dear," Mom says. "You were together, what? Two months?"

"Nearly four!" says Kathy. "I thought he was the one."

Dad sips milk from a glass and wipes his mouth with the back of his hand.

"You're right," he says. "I never really did like him. Just

didn't seem right for you, or that you were happy with him. I just want what's best for you. For you to be happy."

"Thanks, Dad," Kathy says.

"You don't have to rush into this," Mom says. "You're only sixteen. You have so much life ahead of you."

They're all quiet for a moment until Kathy breaks the silence.

"How did you know?" she asks.

"Know what?" asks Mom.

"You know that Dad was the one?" Kathy asks.

Mom looks at Dad.

Dad shrugs.

Mom smiles.

"Frankly, he was the only boy living nearby that I wasn't related to."

"What?" Kathy asks.

"Hey!" says Dad. "That's not entirely true."

"Well, other than that one weird kid, who was always off shooting something or throwing rocks at frogs."

"You have to remember," says Dad. "This farm, our farm, was the only thing around here, for miles. And families stuck together and abutted their properties and helped one another out, so you had a lot of family living around."

"Not like today," says Mom. "Where your aunts and uncles have sold and moved away, and now we have little subdivisions of houses as neighbors."

"And paved roads," says Dad. "Though, I like that. Never really cared for the dirt roads, where you had to worry about kicking up stones or whatever the dirt equivalent of hydroplaning is when you try to stop on a road that's all washboarded."

Mom and Dad smile at one another.

"But what about school?" asks Kathy.

"Sure," says Mom. "There were other kids at school, but Dad had already caught my eye when I was young. I'm not quite sure how he didn't fall into that 'friend zone' or whatever you kids call it, but he didn't. He was always there, and we just clicked."

"Friend zone," Kathy mutters and laughs. "Wow, I had no idea."

"You didn't ask," says Dad. "But, that's the thing. You never know. But when you know, you just know."

"Thank God proximity bias or I wouldn't even be around," says Kathy.

Mom shrugs. "Yeah, there is something to that. The more someone's around, the more you tend to like them."

"Until they give you a reason not to," says Dad.

"Yes," says Mom. She points at dad, "that. That has definitely happened. More than once."

"So, what you're saying is spend time around people until they start to rub off on you?" asks Kathy.

"And avoid the friend zone," says Dad. "Unless you want friends. Then that's fine."

"Friends are good," says Mom. "You need friends in this world."

"Just take your time," says Dad. "No rush. You don't have to have this all figured out before you graduate. Some people take a while, and it's important to get to know yourself, too. Know who you are and what you want."

"Dad's right," Mom says. "It's more important to find the right one than it is to always be in a relationship. Sometimes having a boyfriend or girlfriend can make it hard to hear you think and learn what you really want."

"How do you know?" asks Kathy.

"Didn't we just cover that?" asks Dad.

"No, I mean, if you two got together and always knew, and you lived out here where you didn't have a lot of options around, how do you know the rest of this stuff?"

Mom laughs.

"Oh honey," Mom says. "First, we read books. We hear stories. We listen. We have siblings and friends who didn't figure it out like we did. But, second, our relationship was never perfect."

"Mom took a sabbatical," Dad says.

"Oh, stop calling it that," Mom says.

"What?" asks Kathy.

"I needed to know if he was the right one," Mom says. "And the only way to do that was to try being without him."

"It didn't last long," says Dad.

"Just long enough," says Mom.

"I had no idea," says Kathy.

"Why would you?" asks Mom. "It was long before you were born. We never told you and you didn't ask."

Dad laughs.

"But it all worked out just fine," Dad says.

Michael's flashback:

The image slowly comes into focus of a younger Michael (12) in a middle school cafeteria. He's carrying a tray of what passes for school lunch—pizza (literally dripping with grease), broccoli (that has been steamed to the point of falling to pieces), and a pint-sized carton of chocolate milk. He's tentative as he approaches a lunch table with one open spot. For the last four years of his life, these have been his best friends. That's harder to show in film—unless we had a flashback within a flashback, or a voiceover—but since we're in a book, I can just tell you. These kids, all from the neighborhood—Kyle (12), Jay (13), and Ken (12)—have begun to pull away from Michael in favor of trying to fit in with the cool kids. Sixth grade is a hard year. It's the first year when the different elementary schools merge and you begin to change classes. It doesn't help that puberty is raging and everyone is awkward and self-conscious. Some days, they're still his best friends—just like he remembers them. Others, they're indifferent to his presence. On the worst days, they're bullies trying to show off and put him down.

As he starts to sit, his oldest friend, Kyle, stops him.

"Ut uh," Kyle says. "We're all done eating, time for you to do your thing."

Michael looks at the three trays in front of him, piled ridiculously high everything precariously balanced.

"Oh, okay," Michael says. He takes one tray and begins to walk away.

"No, one trip," says Jay.

"Why?" Michael asks.

"Because he said so," says Ken.

When Michael doesn't react, Ken stands. He is much taller than Michael and has a hint of a mustache.

Michael returns to the table and attempts to stack the trays. Milk spills. A mess is made. He eventually takes all the trays to the trash and returns to eat his lunch.

"Get napkins to clean up your mess, slop," Jay says.

Kyle looks embarrassed for his friend and refuses to make eye contact. He laughs with Jay and Ken, but it's hollow and fake.

Michael walks away, gets napkins, cleans up the mess, throws the napkins away, and returns to eat his lunch. The pizza is covered in chocolate milk. The broccoli is flattened.

"God, you're a mess!" Ken says. He laughs and the rest of the kids at the table join in.

Michael hates messes and works meticulously to clean the mess. He throws away his uneaten lunch and apologizes to the lunch lady for the mess at the table.

When he gets home from school, Michael's father (38) greets him.

"Hey bud," Dad says.

Michael doesn't verbally respond but drops his backpack and runs into Dad's arms.

"Whoa," Dad says and hugs Michael. "Tough day?"

"I don't have any friends!" Michael says through tears.

"What about Kyle, Jay, and that other k-named kid?" Dad asks.

"Ken's the worst!" Michael says.

They stand like that until Michael lets go and pulls away.

"Do you know where Mom is?" Michael asks.

"Oh, you know I don't really keep tabs on her since…" Dad trails off instead of saying the word divorce. ," Dad says. "But she's probably in the air. That's the life of a flight attendant."

We could flash to a map to show Mom (37) flying over the midwest, but there's really no need.

Jenna's flashback:

It's Jenna's 22nd birthday and she's at her parents' house. How do we know it's her 22nd birthday? Well, there's a calendar from 2002 on the wall, which, if this were a movie, the camera would slowly pan by as it ultimately settles and focuses on Jenna, her parents, and the cake they baked for her. No, it does not have 22 candles. Then how do we know it's her 22nd birthday? Hang tight, all will be revealed.

"Wow, that's really…" Jenna pauses as she takes in the cake. "Something."

The cake is vividly, but haphazardly, decorated in neon frosting. The writing is barely legible, but with a little imagination it reads: "Happy Birthday! Jenna!"

"Your mom was up all last night finishing it," Dad (39)

says.

"Not all night," Mom (38) says, blushing. "But I was inspired by that navy blue, velour tracksuit you used to wear. Remember that?"

Jenna does remember. This story comes up more often than she'd like. She smiles and offers a forced laughed, which her parents don't seem to mind.

"Oh my god," Dad says. "You wore that everywhere! In fact, we eventually had to disappear it."

"Dad!" Jenna says.

"What?" Dad says. "It was full of holes and didn't really fit you."

Jenna shakes her head. She's heard this story before, but this is the first time Dad has said "disappear it," which she only recently taught him after one of her Latin American History classes. "Disappearing people is a real thing, it's not something to joke about."

"I'm sorry, honey," Dad says.

"You were heartbroken when it was missing," Mom says. "It was so hard to lie to you. But…" she trails off and goes into the living room out of sight.

This is new, Jenna thinks, but doesn't say it.

Her mother returns and yells, "UNLESS!" She throws the tracksuit at Jenna. It is indeed very reminiscent of the cake frosting.

When Jenna removes the tracksuit from her head, she's crying.

"What? Did I scare you?" Mom asks.

"What's wrong, honey?" Dad asks.

Jenna wipes the tears away and tries to shake them off, but her parents are persistent.

"It's just," Jenna says. "I'm twenty-two!"

Her parents wait patiently for her to say more. But, after a moment of silence, they think maybe that's all there is.

"It's a good age!" says Dad.

"Right!" says Mom. "Gosh, if I could be twenty-two, maybe I could still keep up with you on the tennis court." She laughs.

"No!" says Jenna.

"What then?" her parents say in unison, and can't help but look at one another and laugh, despite the circumstances.

Jenna says.

"It's just," she begins, "just look at me."

"We are, and you look great to us," Dad says.

"You're the perfect daughter," says Mom.

"We love you with all our heart," says Dad.

"I appreciate that," Jenna says. "But don't you think I'm a bit of a… a… fuckup?"

Her parents, again as one, frown at her.

"Why? Why would we even think that?" asks Dad.

"Because by twenty-two, you were done with college, had a kid, and bought a house," says Jenna. "And me, I'm just still struggling through school. I'm not going to be done in four years."

Mom puts her arm around Jenna and hugs her.

"Oh honey," Mom says. "We'd never expect that from you."

"And frankly," says Dad, "being teen parents isn't all it's cracked up to be. Don't get me wrong, I wouldn't have done it any other way, or we wouldn't have you. But…" He pauses. "It's a lot. We made a lot of stupid mistakes and didn't have nearly as much money as we would have liked to, in order to give you all you want and deserve."

"Right," says Mom, taking a seat next to Jenna but remaining close to her. "I mean, we lived on frozen fish sticks for a month or so because they were on sale and that was all we could afford."

Dad laughs.

"But I don't even really have a prospect," says Jenna.

"Prospect for what? Are you mining for gold?" Dad asks.

Jenna frowns at him. "No, for marriage."

Mom and Dad laugh.

"No rush dear," says Mom. "Really. Take. Your. Time. I love your dad and all, and he knows all this, but we really rushed into that because we thought we were doing what was right."

"And," adds Dad, "we ultimately chose to love one another, even when there were times when we weren't sure."

Jenna smiled and ran a finger along the edge of her cake, collecting a small pile of frosting which she enjoyed. She looked to her parents for correction, but neither offered any.

Sensing she was being tested, Mom shrugs and says, "Heck, it's your birthday, you can eat your cake however you want."

"Remember when she put her whole face into her cake?" Dad asks.

"I was four!" says Jenna.

With the flashbacks out of the way, we now return to the story already in progress. You know, where Jenna was waiting to see the Love Formula's updated results of her date with David.

THE LMP

Jenna is sitting at her work desk looking at her laptop, waiting for the formula to update with David's results. She hits F5 repeatedly. Finally, the percentage on the screen changes from 87% to 93%.

"Curse Michael and his stupid LMP!" Jenna dials Michael on her cell phone. It rings twice before Michael answers.

"Jell-O?" he says.

"I just wanted to tell you you're an asshole."

"And to think I went all Bill Cosby on you when I answered the phone."

"You know he's a rapist, right?"

"What?" Michael asks. "Cliff? Dr. Huxtable?"

"I mean, not that he's been formally charged of," Jenna said before adding, "yet. But Wendy Williams said so in the '90s on her radio show, and then there was a Playmate who said something in the late 90s, and just a few years ago, I remember, what was her name? I can't remember, but there were at least two others more recently."

"Oh man," Michael says. "I guess I really should pay more attention to the news. But really, I just meant Jell-O-

Pudding-Pop Bill though, not even stand-up Bill, or Cosby Show Bill. It's a character he was playing. That guy, that character, Jell-O Pudding Pop Guy, was clean and wholesome, right?"

"They're all the same person," Jenna says. "You can't pick and choose."

"It's a hard habit to break," Michael says. "But I'll do better." He pauses for a moment before adding, "So, besides referencing an alleged rapist, why am I an ass again?"

"Your Lowest Match Percentage thingie."

"The LMP? You're not down with LMP? Ya, you know me. What's that got to do with the price of tea in China?"

"Ha ha. Ha. Ha. You're so witty and funny." Jenna rolls her eyes and, though Michael can't see it, he feels the eye roll in the silence. "My match with David went from an eighty-seven to a ninety-three."

"Wait, ninety-three is higher than eighty-seven. That's good, right?"

"Yes. It is higher. And yes, a higher number is better. But on the date, it felt like it should have been higher."

"Maybe you should go with your gut then? Like Kathy. You know she said she's not even going to look at the new percentage before calling Louise back. Maybe you should take a page from her book?"

"Maybe. I just want to know. And your LMP only shows me the lowest match score of the two of us."

"Well, I wouldn't encourage it, but you know how to read the raw data if you really wanted to. Or you could just call the guy and take a chance." Michael busts out into song: "*Take a chance on me...*"

"Stop that singing!" Jenna says, laughing. "Thanks though. Sometimes you're not such an ass. Sometimes you know just what to say."

She disconnects from Michael and dials David.

"Hello?"

David answers. He's in his apartment, which is pretty beige and plain, but dotted here and there with black and white photographs. He's sitting on a black leather couch, working on a laptop on his coffee table. "Hello?"

Now, imagine ABBA's classic "Take a Chance on Me" swells and obscures their conversation. If this were a movie, it would play over a montage. No doubt you're familiar with montages and how they work. It's a quick trick to yada yada over things and show the passage of time. Sometimes they're done with a kind of time-lapse effect, and others you just get clips that fade in and out of one another. You certainly wouldn't get a narrator telling you interesting facts about the song playing during the montage—and they almost always have a song. Like, for instance, the working title for "Take a Chance on Me" was "Billy Boy." Or that one of the two principal songwriters, Bjorn Ulvaeus, was a runner and used the "tck-a-ch"-style rhythm to pace himself as he ran, and this is where the rhythm for the song originates. Maybe you'd want to know that the b-side to the single, was "I'm a Marionette"? No? Not interesting? Okay, let's just let the song play out in your head as I tell you what's happening with David and Jenna.

Here they are at the farmer's market in Kerrytown. They wander, inspecting stalls and talking with farmers and vendors as they go. They aren't thinking that this market has been open and running since 1919, or that these stalls and sheds were built between 1938 and 1940 as part of the New Deal WPA program. The song continues to play as Jenna and David inspect local honey and ask the vendor about the process of harvesting it. They do not stop to wonder why this part of Ann Arbor is called Kerrytown. If they did, they might learn it was named after a lawyer's mother, who was from County Kerry in Ireland. Or that Kerrytown was part of the original village, called Annarbour, and formed in 1833. They smile at the vendor and pay for a bottle of his honey.

Now, an indeterminate number of days later, David and Jenna are on a picnic at the Nichols Arboretum, which sounds fancy, but it's really just a large protected green space. Locals call it "The Arb," and when David first suggested the picnic, that's how he introduced the idea. "Picnic at The Arb?" he asked. But you wouldn't hear that over ABBA's song. You'd just see him mouthing the words.

Now they're back at David's apartment and he's making dinner. Sometimes I wonder, in movies, if they have a specific actual meal they're preparing, so the actor knows what he or she should be doing and how best to pretend to time the meal to all come together at the right time. In this case, David is making roasted vegetables with pesto. He tosses the vegetables in a large plastic tub, the kind of thing chefs use for storage. And in fact, he acquired this tub from a restaurant supply store. David pours in olive oil as he says something to Jenna that makes her laugh. He sprinkles salt and grinds pepper. He puts a lid on the tub, shakes everything together, and then pours the contents on a cooking sheet and slides it into the pre-heated oven.

If the music was playing, you wouldn't be able to hear the conversation. In movies, sometimes they actually have dialogue, and other times they're just saying things like, "peas and carrots" to make it look like they're having a conversation, since they know the music will ultimately obscure it. In this case, we can zoom in and hear what they're talking about, because while the song is likely looped in your head, I can transcribe their conversation here.

"How did a guy so interested in art, end up with such a bland-looking apartment?" Jenna asks.

"Hey! Art comes in all kinds of shapes and sizes," David responds. "Just because it's black and white photography on the walls doesn't mean it's not aesthetically pleasing and beautiful."

"I don't disagree," Jenna says. "But the walls are so beige and bland. It looks, if you don't mind me saying so, rather generic and like you're not planning on staying long."

"Well, you never know. I mean, I'm not in a rush to go anywhere, and working at the art museum is really my dream job. But it doesn't hurt to live light."

"Do you have a jumpbag ready to go in your closet?"

David laughs.

"No," he says. "But I do like to travel when I can. Plus, you know, this is an apartment. I don't own it, it's not like I can just paint the walls whatever I want."

"You can if you repaint it before you move out," Jenna says. She's pacing around his living room, inspecting the photography. Before David can respond again, she asks, "Are these yours?"

"Some of them are," David says. "You can probably tell which ones."

"So, how did you come to love art so much?" Jenna asks, looking at the photography, trying to figure out which David might have taken and which were "professional." She can't tell.

"My mom and dad always had art around. Never fancy stuff, but things they'd pick up at art fairs or from local artists," David says as plucks leaves of basil from a small plant growing in his kitchen. He drops the leaves into a food processor as he goes on. "It's definitely not because I'm an artist. I mean, I can draw a little, but nothing like," he gestures into the air. "Maybe that's why? Because I don't understand how someone can do it. It drives me to keep trying to figure it out."

Jenna stops her perusal of the photography and turns to look at him. She nods.

Pretend the music swells again, and now they're at the art museum again. What happened to dinner? Oh, it was fine, they had a good night, but we cut the meal for time. It didn't really add to the story. David is sitting next to Jenna on a bench in front of Ivan Generalic's "Deer in the Forest" (1956). Something is captivating about the image. They stare at it and don't talk.

Now they're at Domino's Farms petting zoo. Yes, this is associated with the pizza corporation. Oddly enough, Domino's owns a herd of bison and a petting zoo. David and Jenna watch baby goats run and jump.

David and Jenna are at Meijer, shopping for groceries. Meijer is another Michigan institution. Those unfamiliar with it might compare it to Target or Walmart, but neither is fair. Meijer is its own thing. Jenna is riding on the front of the shopping cart, while David pushes her wildly through the store.

And here they are at Jerusalem Garden, eating falafels with hummus just like Jenna's first time at the restaurant. David's smiling and enjoying his meal, and Jenna's nodding approvingly. Now she's sharing her tabbouli and he's asking for more. David's pointing at baklava on the menu, but Jenna's shaking her head. She's saying, "too obvious" even though you can't hear the words over the music. Instead, she's ordering mamoul and grabia—the former being a delicious, sweet pastry stuffed with walnuts, pistachios, and dates, and the latter being a flaky, buttery cookie; Jenna can never choose between them, so she almost always orders both. And now, after a quick cut, the dessert has arrived and they're obviously enjoying the treats and licking their fingers.

Finally, here's the last scene of the montage: David and Jenna, kissing, leaning up against the wall in Jenna's apartment, next to the Miro. The music ends, and so does this chapter.

CATCHING UP WITH THE OTHERS

Since the last chapter dealt so exclusively with Jenna and David, I figured it was only fair to report on how the others are doing. If you haven't figured it out, Jenna is kind of our "main character," but, were this a movie, it would be referred to as having "a great ensemble cast." So it's important we give them a chance to shine as well.

Jenna's absence at Tree Town was certainly noticed. Not that she couldn't have fit a trip to the coffee shop into her schedule, but she just didn't. David was shiny and new, and things were going great, so she rode that wave instead. Michael and Kathy continued to meet, perform the necessary maintenance on the Love Formula, answer emails, and, in general, carry on.

On this day in particular, Michael is on his way to Tree Town when he receives a text from Kathy.

Running late, can you just come to Louise's?

Interesting, Michael thinks. He hadn't been to Louise's place yet.

Sure, he types. *Address?*

The response comes in, and he realizes it isn't even very far to walk.

On my way.

A few minutes and blocks later, he arrives at a house. He stands back to marvel at it. It's a legit home. Not an apartment or condo or townhouse, but an actual house. With an actual yard. He knows that Louise is older, but somehow hasn't put age together with the acquisition of wealth and the possibility of owning a house. He walks up and knocks on the door.

Louise answers.

"Come in," she says and gives him a short hug as entered.

He looks around. Yes, this was most definitely an actual house with adult furniture and decorations.

"Wow," he says.

"What?" Louise asks. "Oh, Kathy will be right down."

Michael notices there are stairs leading up. There was even more actual-house to this actual house than he had at first realized.

"Just," he says at a loss, "I really like your space."

"Oh?" Louise asks. "Thanks. It's just a few things that I've acquired from travels and around and whatever."

Now Michael actually looked at the decorations.

"Is that a framed copy *of The Downward Spiral?*" he asks.

Louise laughs.

"It is! And," Louise lowers her voice and leans in toward Michael conspiratorially, "it's even signed."

"No-fucking-way," he walks over to it and inspects it. "How?" he asks, slightly embarrassed that he was reduced to "wow" and "how" and other single-syllable words.

"It's a funny story," Louise says. She looks to see if Kathy is on her way and, when she determines she has time, she begins again. "Well, I know you're all younger than me, so you might not remember this, but some of the record stores used to stay open to midnight to do a record release sale."

Michael wanted to say he remembered this, because he wanted to fit in, but in fact he did not remember record stores staying open until midnight.

"I went because I wanted the new Soundgarden album," Louise says, "I was a big fan *Badmotorfinger* and *Louder Than Love*."

"Really?" Michael asks. "I didn't peg you for a grunge-chick."

"Eww," Louise says, scrunching up her nose. She repeats, "grunge-chick."

Michael laughs.

"You probably didn't realize I went to raves or goth clubs either then," she says, laughing at the memory. "But, anyway, I went with a bunch of friends who were into NIN. I knew NIN—from aforementioned goth clubs—but I wasn't a huge fan."

"Then why do you have that?" Michael asks, pointing at the album behind glass hanging on the wall.

"I'm getting there," Louise says. "The three or four of us went and waited in line. At midnight the two albums went on sale. To help promote the album, Discount Records had a raffle for a vinyl version of *The Downward Spiral*."

"No way," Michael says. "You won it?"

Louise laughs. "When they called me, I thought it was a joke. Since I didn't even buy the CD that night. I bought *Superunknown*."

Michael shakes his head. "That's crazy."

"Crazier still," Louise says, "Trent came to do an in-store event at Tower Records and I managed to get him to sign it. I told him the story, about how I didn't even really like the band that much and managed to win the album, and he thought it was the funniest thing he'd heard."

"You told him that?"

"I did," Louise says. "But it probably helped that I told him he had won me over with *The Downward Spiral.*"

Michael and Louise break into laughter just as Kathy emerges from upstairs.

"What'd I miss?" she asks.

"Don't worry," Louise says, tucking a stray hair behind Kathy's ear. "I'll tell you later. Right now, can I get either of you coffee? I understand I'm no Conrad, but I do have the ability to brew up some bean juice."

"Eww, bean juice really belittles the joy that is coffee," Michael says.

"I think he means, yes please," Kathy says.

The three of them move into the kitchen. Michael and Kathy sit, while Louise grinds beans and brews coffee.

"So, how's it going with Charlie?" Kathy asks.

"Good," Michael says. "At least today."

"Up and down?" asks Kathy.

"I want to make a joke there," Michael says, "but I'm going to refrain. I need to call out moments like this, so you realize I'm maturing and can actualize self-control. Sometimes."

"That's good to know," Kathy says. "That you're growing into an adult, however delayed that might be. But, to my question?"

"Oh," Michael says. "Yes. Up and down. Sometimes it feels like we click, and then suddenly we don't."

Louise joins them at the table as the coffee begins to brew.

"Any commonality between when you don't?" she asks.

"Probably me," Michael says. He thinks for a moment and then adds, "Mostly me. Being dumb. Saying the wrong thing. Overthinking something."

"Well," Louise says, "at least you're being yourself. And

Charlie knows what she's getting into. Nothing worse than wearing a mask and pretending to be something you're not."

Kathy nods.

"There's no point in pretending," Kathy says. "You just prolong the reveal that you're not put together and perfect."

Louise smiles and nods at Kathy.

"Besides," Kathy says, "there's a kind of beauty in imperfection and vulnerability."

"That's the second time I've heard that about vulnerability."

"Oh?" asks Kathy.

Michael frowns and says, "Yeah, Charlie said something about vulnerability being sexy."

"I think you should probably listen," says Louise, getting up from the chair. "She's telling you what she needs."

"And she's right," says Kathy.

Louise places steaming mugs in front of Michael and Kathy and then returns for hers.

Michael blows gently on the steam.

"So, how is it going with—" Michael gestures with his head in the direction of Louise "—you know."

Kathy and Louise both laugh.

"I know, it's a stupid question," Michael says. "I mean, just look at you two. Hanging out in a grown-up house, being all adorable and supportive of one another." He turns his gaze to Kathy. "And you, staying over."

Kathy blushes.

"When you know, you just know," says Louise.

"But, how do you know you just know?" Michael asks. "I mean, Charlie is so different from anyone else I've been with, but I don't know, you know?"

"Louise isn't wrong," Kathy says. "But more than just knowing, just because it's the right person, doesn't mean it isn't work. You have to work at it. You have to choose love."

"You both do," Louise adds.

Michael sighs. "You sound like love-Yodas, I swear."

"Is that a thing?" Louise asks.

"If it wasn't before, it is now," Kathy says, laughing.

"Choose you must. Love is work it is," Michael says, doing a terrible Yoda impression. "But, really, sometimes I'm just afraid of revealing all of who I am. There's a lot. You know? I mean, I know I can be a lot. I don't want to scare her."

"I don't think you're going to scare her away," says Kathy. "I know you. Yes, you're a lot, but you're not more than someone can handle."

"It often takes both you and Jenna," says Michael.

Kathy laughs.

"But," Louise says, "she's been gone for a couple days now, almost a week, and look, Kathy's been holding down the fort."

"With your help!" Michael says, laughing.

"If she's the right one," says Kathy, "it will be fine. If she's not, then I don't think a matter of days or weeks or months is going to make her any more ready for the full-Michael."

"The full-Michael," Michael echoes. "That sounds gross, and I'm Michael."

I could hang out here and listen to them chat, but it's important to know when to cut away.

HISTORY OF RAYS

Each of the Love Formula team members are working independently. Periodically, they contribute to the group-text. It's almost like being in the office—or coffee shop—together. Jenna's working on a spreadsheet, crunching numbers. Michael is tweaking some of the code. And Kathy is responding to emails. No one has addressed Jenna's disappearance from their typical friend group gatherings. Until now.

So, everything okay with David? Kathy texts.

Yeah, why? Jenna replies.

Just… feels like we haven't seen you much, Kathy replies.

I'm right here, Jenna texts.

She's right, you've disappeared into Davidville, population 2, Michael replies.

Things have been going great, Jenna types, then adds, *sorry.*

Just wanted to make sure. Just remember, it's all about balance, Kathy types.

You don't want to smother him. I've done that before, it's not good, Michael replies.

I'm not smothering him, Jenna types. Then she mutters to herself, "I haven't gone anywhere."

Okay, glad to have you back, Kathy types.

They continue working on their projects and it seems as if the group text is going to end there, but Kathy disrupts the digital silence.

OMG! Kathy sends.

What? Jenna replies.

WE WON! Kathy texts.

Who? What? Who won what? Jenna types.

The hotdog thing? Michael replies. When no one replies, he types, *Rays? Or whatever? That contest you and Louise entered?*

What? What's that? Jenna sends.

Something you missed while visiting Davidville. Kathy and Louise entered a contest to write a history for the hotdog place they love, Michael types.

YES! It's live" Kathy types.

Then Kathy responds with the url, and Michael and Jenna click almost at the same time, across town from one another. Were this a film, you'd probably get a two-way, or even three-way, split of their reactions as they read in unison. Perhaps a voiceover would read it for the benefit of the viewer—because, you know, it'd be hard to read this much text on the screen. It's certainly more than a *Star Wars* crawl. Here, you'll just have to imagine they're reading in unison.

In order for one empire to rise to the top, another must fall. Think the: Mongol Empire, Russian Empire, Yuan Dynasty, Qing Empire, Holy Roman Empire, German Empire, Macedonian Empire, Xin Dynasty, Byzantine Empire, Ottoman Empire, etc. As such, the history of Ray's Red Hots is tightly enmeshed with the history of the previous Red Hot Empire: Red Hot Lovers. And the history of Red Hot Lovers, not so different from the Ottoman Empire, begins with a Turk.

Picture Indiana Jones. No, not *Last Crusade,* not *Temple of Doom.* I'm talking *Raiders of the Lost Ark.* Remember the shady Turkish guy with the eyepatch? The one with the dark mustache and shaggy goatee? The one who poisons the dates in an attempt to kill Indiana and/or Marion (the love interest)? The one with the monkey? Remember the sad scene where the monkey eats the poisoned dates instead? Remember the shady café? First of all, never trust a man with an eyepatch (unless it's on National Talk like a Pirate Day), let alone a man with shady facial hair. That's just good advice for any occasion. Now, keep that image of the Turk in mind.

Shift to sometime in the mid-90s. Maybe 94? 95? It was post-Cobain suicide that's for sure. Picture a dark computer lab on North Campus. An Engineering computer lab. Sun computers abound. It's dark inside. I have just been introduced to a Turk named Deniz. "What?" Deniz. "What's a Deniz?" Not what, but who. Deniz Demir. He wasn't wearing an eyepatch, but he shared some of the shady facial hair qualities of the Indiana Jones villain, and he had wavy hair. He was swarthy. I tentatively trusted him as he had let me into the computer lab in the first place.

The Deniz suggested: "Let's go get some food." Who could deny that kind of wisdom? Food is always good. "There's this great hotdog place…" Wait, I don't do hotdogs. Besides, who goes "out" for hotdogs? "No, seriously, these aren't just hotdogs. They're red hots." What the hell is a red hot? (I'm picturing the spicy cinnamon candy.) "Trust me," he said with a wink. I can't help but picture the shady Turk using the monkey as a distraction while he pours the poison on the dates. I was leery and suspicious. But that would be my trump card. I would play his little game, but I would be cautious. Plus, I had another friend along. I'd let him try the food first and if he didn't die… then I'd risk it.

Once there I was put at ease. These weren't just hotdogs. These were all natural casing pure beef red hots. Plus, the Chicago Dog, Serious Dog, Reuben Dog, etc all offered plenty of toppings to cover up the taste of a hotdog if you weren't a fan of the typical Ball Park Frank—and, I wasn't. I watched cautiously as my friends ordered. "What? Four bucks for a hotdog? Are you fucking kidding me?" The Turk put my fears at ease. He would buy. "Very well then." I tried them and fell in love. Four dollars, or $3.50, or whatever the price was, was well worth it. This was a special, special place. The atmosphere was funky. College kids ran the place. There was always some kind of weird music playing—usually stuff I enjoyed. You could eat outside at these little patio tables, or inside at the tables with benches. The walls were decorated with all kinds of things Chicago-related. Newspapers, prints, posters, etc. It quickly became a favorite.

Years passed; I moved away from the state, but whenever I came home, I made a point of stopping by for my favorites: Serious Dog and Chicago Dog. The Reuben Dog was a close third, but I was trying to watch my weight. I noticed new items on the menu: tofu dogs, burgers, vegetarian options, etc. Life got busy and I came to the restaurant less and less.

Eventually, more years had passed since I had had my favorite culinary treats. A friend, the very friend who accompanied me on the initial visit with the Turk, emailed me and said Red Hot Lovers was no more. A sad day. "But!" he said, "A new empire has arisen from the ashes, like a fiery phoenix!" Ray's Red Hots. A few tweaks to the menu, for instance, the Serious Dog is now the Slaw Dog, but otherwise: same location, same great food, same great atmosphere. They just need a historian. Someone to describe their humble beginnings and get people caught up to the current day. Merging the past with the present. Raising the banner of the new empire and blaring the trumpets to announce the change of the guard. A NEW DAY HAS COME. BEHOLD:

RAY'S RED HOTS.

They're not just hot dogs. Good food. Trust me. Enjoy.

"Wow," says Jenna, in her living room, sitting on the couch, with her laptop on the coffee table in front of her. She laughs and leans back against the back of the couch and picks up her phone, contemplating what to say.

"Wow," says Michael, in his bedroom, sitting on the floor, with his laptop sprawled out before him. He picks up his phone and responds, *wow!*

Jenna replies: *you took the word right out of my mouth.*

Kathy replies: *you like it?*

Michael replies: it was funny and very compelling. I didn't get bored at all.

Kathy replies: *high praise.*

Jenna replies: *so, what now?*

Kathy replies: *Ray is buying us lunch to thank us.*

Michael replies: *us, us? Or do you mean you and Louise, us?*

Kathy replies: *Louise and me. We co-wrote it.*

Michael replies: *well, that makes more sense.*

Jenna replies: *congratulations! I'm with Michael, that was really funny. I love it. Sometimes I forget that you're a great writer.*

Kathy replies: *thanks. I appreciate it.*

Michael replies: *I feel like there's a joke in here, about lesbians loving a hotdog place.*

Jenna replies: no.

Michael replies: *but.*

Jenna replies: *no.*

Kathy replies: *okay, gotta run, but just had to share!*

CHEMISTRY ALL AROUND

Sometimes in a movie, or book, there are scenes that echo one another. They're not quite a repeat or rehash of the same tread, but instead, maybe it's a character in the same situation but a different setting. Or maybe it almost feels like déjà vu. These aren't accidental or a sign of the creative person being lazy but are intentionally meant to hold up a mirror to allow the reader, or viewer, to see if the reflection matches the image. Or maybe there's something just off. Not so different from the images popular in children's magazines, like *Highlights*, where you are asked to spot the differences between two images. In either case, all this is to say this is one such chapter. The mirror image appears later. Of course, it's not exactly the same and, in fact, maybe it is a collection of moments that are reflective here, but you'll know it when you read it. I'll leave it at that.

David walks into Tree Town and approaches the counter.

Conrad finishes drying a coffee mug and nods at his approach.

"Hey," David says. He glances up and down the specials board. "What do you recommend?"

"Well, I am admittedly biased," Conrad says.

"As the owner and all," David adds.

"Right," Conrad smiles. "But I happen to think the most expensive latte on the menu is the best thing we have to offer."

David laughs.

"Just because it's the most expensive?" he asks.

Conrad shrugs.

"I mean, yeah, but it's also expensive for a reason."

"Like gold leaf floating on the foam?" David asks.

"Not a bad idea," Conrad says, miming writing it down for later use. "In truth, just depends what you want. Today's roast is a fantastic roast from Hawaii."

"Where from?" David asks.

"Hawaii," Conrad answers.

"No, I mean, which farm?" David asks.

"Oh, sorry," Conrad digs for a bag of beans. "Greenwell."

"No kidding? I toured there when I visited a couple years ago," David says.

"Really? Cool place?" Conrad asks. "I mean, I love their coffee, but I've never visited. I went to Oahu once for a friend's wedding, but never to the Big Island."

"Oh yeah, it's amazing. Plus, Greenwell has a huge variety of fruit trees and avocado trees all over the property."

"I'll have to check it out," Conrad says. "I'm trying to do a better job of finding that illusive work-life balance everyone's talking about."

David nods. "I hear it's hard to get that balance just right. But it probably helps when you're an entrepreneur like you. I mean, first Tree Town Records, now the coffee shop?"

Conrad laughs. "I guess. I mean, the record company

went belly-up, so we probably shouldn't use that as a metric to measure anything. And the coffee house has me here longer than I'd like to be."

"You just need some new staff," David says.

"I am looking," Conrad says and adds. "If you know anyone."

"It just so happens, that this guy named Cosmo said he was looking for a job," David says. He flips through his phone for the contact. "He was saying he needed something less corporate. More laid back."

Conrad looks around and nods.

"Here," David says. "Got something to write his number down?"

Conrad pulls a pad from his apron and jots down the number as David reads it to him.

"Thanks for that," Conrad says. "If it pans out, I'll spot you a free super expensive latte. In the meanwhile, what can I get for you today?"

"I just want a mug of the Greenwell Coffee, you got me jonesing for it," David says.

"Figures," Conrad says, shrugging. He pours the coffee and slides the mug to David.

"Thanks," David pays and steps back from the counter. He looks around.

"Looking for someone?" Conrad asks.

"Yeah, a group of friends," David says.

Before he can say Jenna's name, Conrad says, "Up on the three."

David looks at him, puzzled, but then smiles and heads for the stairs.

On three, he finds the whole group sitting at their usual table. It's the largest table and the only one of its kind. Most of the tables are built for two or four; the preferred one can accommodate six easily, eight with a little squishing. Today, no squishing is required. Charlie and Michael sit on one end, Kathy and Jenna are in the middle, and Louise is sitting next to Kathy. There's an empty seat for David next to Jenna.

"Alright, now the gang's all here," Michael says. He stands and greets David with a handshake. "You must be David."

"Michael, right?" David asks, returning the handshake.

"Bingo."

Kathy and Louise all stand in turn and greet him. Jenna smiles and waits for him to sit.

"So," David trails off. "Now what? I don't see a swinging light nor a polygraph, so it can't be an interrogation."

The group laughs and Jenna softly punches him in the arm.

"No, not an interrogation, but we can definitely identify some pitfalls to save you both some time and suffering," Kathy says, she extends her hand. "Hand me your iPod."

Jenna starts to say something, but Kathy cuts her off.

"Nope, you've spent however many weeks with this guy now, this is our turn to get to know him." She opens and closes her extended hand. "iPod please."

"How do you even know that I have one? Or that it would be on me?" asks David.

"If you didn't, and it wasn't, then that would already be a sign," Kathy says, smiling.

David reaches into his pocket, retrieves the little device, and hands it to Kathy.

Kathy clicks and scrolls.

"Interesting," she says.

"What?" Michael and Jenna say at almost the same time.

Louise is rolling her eyes. "It feels a bit like a violation, doesn't it?" she asks.

"A bit," says David.

"Well," Kathy says. "He has a playlist for *Some Girls* by the Rolling Stones."

"A playlist instead of just playing the album?" Michael asks.

"I just find it easier to keep all the music I listen to in playlists," David says.

Michael eyes him. "Interesting. Also, interesting album choice. Your favorite of theirs?"

"Yeah, I probably am supposed to like *Beggars* or *Exile* or *Sticky Fingers* or even *Satanic Majesties*, but I love *Some Girls*. I can't help it."

Kathy nods. "It is a good one. Underappreciated." She pauses and hums.

"What?" asks Jenna.

"A playlist named 'Love'," Kathy says.

"What's on it?" Jenna asks, trying to see over the table.

"Queen, Journey, Foreigner, U2, Boston, Cyndi Lauper," Kathy rattles them off. "Fleetwood Mac?"

"I don't know that I'd associate love with them, they were such an incestuous drug-fueled mess," Louise agrees.

"If you remove yourself from the context of when the songs were written, and who they were written about," David says, "then you can appreciate the songs are love songs."

"Doesn't look like any Beatles on here," Michael says.

Jenna gasps.

"I debated about 'Something'," David says, "but this wasn't intended to be an all-inclusive list of music."

"Wait," Kathy says, "'Maybe I'm Amazed' is on here."

"That's a Paul song," David says, "and the Wings."

Michael, Kathy, and Jenna all smile and nod at David.

"What about November Rain?" asks Charlie.

"That music video kind of spoiled the song for me," says David.

"So context and all that does matter some times?" Charlie asks, laughing.

David bows his head, acknowledging the fair point.

"Nope," says Kathy.

"Nope what?" asks Louise.

Michael and Jenna nod and wait eagerly for a response as well.

"Led Zeppelin," says Kathy.

"As in, there isn't enough?" asks Louise.

Kathy frowns at her. "Really? No, in this case, he has included the song 'Whole Lotta Love,' and well, I rest my case."

"How?" asks Michael. "I mean, it literally has 'love' in the title."

"It has that whole breakdown section where Robert Plant is grunting and making sex noises for entirely too long. *Ewww.* I don't need that."

"How long is too long?" Michael asks.

"No song needs sex noises," says Charlie. "I agree with Kathy there."

"Enough about music," Charlie says. "What else should we know about you? I didn't really get this kind of rapid-fire opportunity, but I'm kind of enjoying it."

David laughs. "I work at the art museum. I like art? Photography. Clearly music as well."

"Favorite movie of the year?" Charlie asks.

The rest of the group ping-pong their heads back and forth between David and Charlie.

"I do like movies, so that's a tough one. Uhm," David considers for a moment. "It's not going to win any of the critics over, but I really loved *Scott Pilgrim vs. the World.*"

The table goes silent.

"What?" David asks. "It was a really inventive way of thinking about relationships."

"I don't think any of us saw it," says Michael. "I mean," he looks at his friends, "correct me if I'm wrong."

No one does.

"Okay," David says. "So, Scott Pilgrim loves this woman, Ramona, but she has ex-boyfriends. He's initially off-put by the perceived baggage and has to grow to learn he has his own baggage and that you have to overcome worrying about that in order to have a successful relationship. If you're always looking back and comparing, then you don't appreciate what's in front of you and what's happening today."

"I thought it was the movie that was like a video game come to life," says Louise.

"It is also that," says David. "Scott Pilgrim literally battles Ramona's ex-boyfriends to defeat her past, but it's really about him overcoming his own obsession with her past."

"Sounds like a romantic comedy," says Michael.

"Something wrong with rom-coms?" asks David.

"No," says Michael. "Frankly, I love a good *Sweet Home Alabama* or *Forgetting Sarah Marshall.*"

"Oh, bold choices," David says. "What about you? He turns to Kathy, Louise, and Charlie. Favorite rom-coms?"

Charlie immediately offers, "*Bridget Jones.*" She shrugs. "Probably predictable, but I love it."

"*My Big Fat Greek Wedding*, because it reminds me so much of my own family," says Louise. "Kathy hasn't met them yet. When you do, bring the Windex."

Everyone laughs.

"I really love the heart and soul of *Hitch*," says Kathy. "But as far as a favorite, probably it would have to be *Sleepless in Seattle* or *You've Got Mail.*"

"An Ephron fan," says David, nodding. "Such classics."

"What about you?" asks Charlie.

"He already said *Scott Pilgrim*," says Michael.

"No, he said that was his favorite film of the year, and you said it sounded like a rom-com," Charlie corrects him. "But he didn't specify it was his favorite rom-com."

"Hard to pick a favorite," says David. "And I guess it depends how generous you're going to be with the genre. I mean, is *Groundhog Day* a rom-com?"

Jenna opens her mouth to speak but, after a quick look from Kathy, she holds her tongue.

The table is silent, waiting for David to explain.

"It's all about love and trying to get it right," David says. "I mean, it's only when Phil finally gives up and stops trying to anticipate every possible outcome and lets his guard down, that he and Rita really connect and the nightmare loop is over."

"Jesus," says Michael. "You really should consider writing reviews for the studios. You sold me on watching that movie again."

"But, if I had to choose," says David. "I'd probably go with *Love Actually*. Even though it's kind of cheating because it's like eight mini rom-coms rolled into one."

The group laughs and smiles.

"Lately though, I'm feeling a bit *Notting Hill*," he laughs. "Because I'm the schmuck commoner following around this huge celebrity. I mean, she was on TV after all and developed this world-famous dating service thing."

"Hey," Kathy says, "we had something to do with that, too!"

"*Legally Blonde* or *Fever Pitch*," says Conrad, from behind the group.

Everyone pivots to look at him.

"Kind of late to the game," Michael says.

"How long have you been hanging out, creeper?" asks Kathy.

Conrad laughs. "I just flit about here and there and figured I'd join in." He waves and wanders back down the stairs.

"So?" David asks. "Am I accepted?"

"We'll have to confer for a final ruling," says Michael. He looks at the others. "But I think we can at least grant you a temporary membership."

NEUROSES

Time has passed; we're now squarely into March of 2011. Yes, that means some potentially interesting scenes have taken place. I mean, there could have been a whole New Year's moment with kisses at midnight—that certainly would have been on brand for The Love Formula—but it's been done before in any number of movies and books. So, instead, we skip ahead and let the characters catch us up. Contextually, you'll be up to speed in no time.

Jenna and Kathy are sitting around a table on the third floor of Tree Town Coffee overlooking State Street and watching students pass by. Michael climbs the stairs and comes into view, carrying a mug of coffee. He joins them at the table.

"Hey stranger," says Kathy. "I guess Charlie's got something that we don't?"

"Definitely something you don't got, er, rather, an orientation that you don't got anyway." Michael smiles and takes a sip from his drink.

"How is she?" Jenna asks.

Michael looks down at the floor and considers his

words carefully. "Things were going really well…"

"Were?" asks Jenna.

"And then?" asks Kathy.

"Until?" asks Jenna.

"I stayed over at her place last night," says Michael.

"That's usually a good thing," says Kathy. "Isn't it?" She looks at Jenna.

Jenna nods. "I thought so?"

"Sure, and it was. It just started out better than it ended," Michael says.

"Explain?"

"Like I said, I went over there last night."

There's a knock on the door and Charlie opens it. Michael enters carrying a bottle of wine in one hand and a 40-ounce in a brown paper bag in the other.

"I wasn't sure exactly what kind of girl you were," he says.

"You don't know yet?" Charlie mocks surprise, grabbing the 40-ounce. "Please tell me this is Olde English!"

Michael silently mouths the word "yes" when she's not looking.

"Classy," says Kathy, interrupting the story.

"I know, she's my kind of girl. Anyway. She made dinner. We ate dinner, drank the 40-ounce, had some wine, sat on the couch, made out for a while, we got naked—"

"I think we get the idea," says Jenna. "We don't need the play-by-play."

"Right," says Kathy, nodding. "So far everything sounds like it's going well. Where's the SNAFU?"

"I'm getting to it. But I think I need to explain something first," Michael pauses before adding, "I have some, quirks."

"They're called neuroses," says Jenna, "and we're well aware of them."

Kathy nods and rolls her eyes. "We've known each other for how long, and you think you've kept something like this from us? Mr. Twitchy?"

"I call them quirks, sure, whatever," Michael says. "One thing is, I don't sleep naked. I always have something on. Underwear, shorts, something."

"Oooookay," says Kathy. "Not something I guess I needed to know, or hear, but I'm assuming this is relevant for some reason?"

"Also, probably not the strangest quirk of yours that I know about," says Jenna.

"Look, do you want to hear this or not? You did ask what happened after all," says Michael.

"Of course, we care and want to hear," says Jenna. "But you should know that sometimes people say that kind of thing out of politeness and kindness, and they don't really want or need to hear about what you wear to bed."

"Fair point," says Michael. "So noted."

"But, again," says Kathy. "Not in this instance. We're here for you."

"Thank you for that." Michael looks at his friends, who nod for him to continue, he takes a drink of his coffee and begins anew. "It's not just a neurosis, to use your word, there's a phobia, too. Of bugs." He raises his hand, anticipating interjections and cuts his friends off. "Now, before you even say anything, or make some joke, or whatever, just shut up. This might be TMI, but it's necessary. You're my friends, I need to be able to talk to you about whatever. So, here it is. You're in the circle of trust. All the way. There's no turning back. Groovy?"

"Absolutely," says Kathy.

"Can it be a triangle of trust? It's just that we have three—" says Jenna, who stops when Michael glares at her.

"I hate bugs. Hate, hate, hate," says Michael. "Really hate. They like moist places. I watch a lot of Discovery and Animal Planet. Probably too much. Anyway, I feel, uhm, comforted. That's the right word. Comforted by wearing something, hell even having a sheet or some kind of cover, to protect my, uhm, warm places and openings. If you get my drift."

"Disturbingly so," says Jenna.

The looks from Kathy and Jenna confirm that they do and the disgust on their faces suggests they would rather not have any additional details about this particular part of the story.

"So, we're naked. We do our thing and then we're laying there. She's kind of on top of me and she falls asleep. I'm naked. My underwear is in the living room. I look for a sheet. Surely, she has a sheet. No sheet. No comforter. No nothing."

"Nothing at all?" asks Jenna. "What kind of bed was this?"

"I don't know! What do I know about beds?" says Michael. "It had a mattress, it looked normal. It was a bed. But, when we ended up on the bed, I wasn't exactly paying attention to the sheet situation. Because I assumed we'd get up and go the bathroom, maybe brush our teeth, or something. But, she just kind of passed out on me."

"Wait," says Kathy. "Is this the first time you guys have done it? Why didn't you know about her sleeping habits and lack of sheets? Also, is she narcoleptic? What's the deal with her passing out right away? You should take her in to get looked at, just in case. That can be a serious condition."

"I'm going to ignore most of those questions," says Michael. "But, no, this was just the first time we'd 'done it', to use your words, in her apartment. And I just didn't think it would be an issue. I mean, who doesn't have sheets?"

"Apparently Little Miss Forty Ounce," says Jenna.

"Apparently," echoes Michael.

"So, that's it? That was the deal breaker?" asks Kathy. "You couldn't ask her to invest in some sheets and move on?"

"Well, there's more."

Charlie is draped over Michael who is lying on his back. He pokes her gently.

"Charlie," he begins quietly. "Charlie? Charlie!" He's not quite yelling, but almost. Michael shakes her and she begins to stir.

"What?" she asks. "What is it?" She looks around, startled, rubbing sleep from her eyes. "Everything okay?"

"I'm cold."

"Cold? I keep it at seventy-eight in here. You're crazy," says Charlie. "Go back to sleep."

"I'm just a little chilly," says Michael.

"I'm not hot enough for you?" Charlie asks. "Here," she says as she moves so she's covering more of Michael's body. "There. Better?"

Before Michael can answer, Charlie's soundly asleep.

"I'm serious about getting her checked out," says Kathy. "But really, you could have just told her about the bug thing. Or even just asked for a blanket. Be more specific and forthright about your needs."

"Seriously? We haven't been together long enough to tell her about the bug thing. I've known you for how long, and you're just finding out about this now?"

"Well," says Jenna. "Neither of us are trying to sleep with you. It seems like 'need to know' information, and like she might need to know it."

"Whatever. So, obviously I didn't sleep at all. I kept feeling things crawling all over my body. Sometimes it was her hair or a pube poking me. Sometimes I couldn't figure out what it was, which really wasn't good for my anxiety. I watched the sun rise behind the blinds of her bedroom. I watched the digital lines on the clock change from four to five to six to seven to eight to nine. She moved now and then, and I thought for sure she'd fully wake up. Surely this would be the move that wakes her up. This is the time. At nine-thirty, I started to cough quietly. By ten I was coughing louder and more often. She didn't seem to notice. Ho well did I know this girl anyway? How could I love someone who slept in until noon? My bladder was announcing that it was full. Very, very full. I tried to shoot laser beams into her skull with my eyes. You know how you can usually make someone look at you if you stare at them? Didn't work. But finally, she woke up."

"Hey cutie," Charlie says. "How did you sleep?"
"Fine. A little tired, but I'm okay."
Charlie smiles at him and rolls off the bed.

"I mean, what else was I going to say? Honesty is the basis of relationships, right? But saying that I didn't sleep a wink because I feared bugs in her bed seemed like a truth worth omitting.

"I must have worn you out," says Charlie. "I'll be right back. I have to use the ladies' room." She stands up and begins a slow walk down the hallway. She looks back over her shoulder and winks at Michael.

Mentally, Michael is in a check-out line with four customers in front of him. He has six items in his basket.

Each of the other customers has carts full of products. On either side of this register are three unmanned registers. As Michael looks around the store, he sees clerks idly standing by, some straightening items on a shelf, others talking to one another. The moment he's the next customer in line, a cashier suddenly appears at the register immediately to his right.

"I'm open," the cashier says.

Michael sadly looks at his items already on the conveyor belt. Another customer, who has just arrived, slides into position at the newly-opened register.

The customer looks at Michael, laughs, and says, "must be my lucky day!"

Michael watches as Charlie saunters into the bathroom and closes the door.

"Yep," he says to his friends at Tree Town, "I've had to go for hours. Hours! And my girlfriend is the dick who just happens to stroll to lane three at just the right time."

"So, you dumped her because she pissed before you did?" asks Jenna.

"Almost," he says. "I mean, what am I? Part camel? It's not like I have a hump that I store extra urine in. Don't most people have to piss in the morning? Especially after drinking?"

"Ladies first?" says Kathy. "I mean, and it's her place. In fairness, she didn't know you'd been awake all night. A normal person might have slid out from under the person sleeping on top of them and found their way to the bathroom, or secured a sheet, or found their underwear."

Michael frowned at Kathy.

"Okay?" says Kathy. "So, what happened then?"

"I practically sprinted to the bathroom, that's what. And while I was going, I was kind of looking around."

"Guys are so gross," says Jenna.

"Don't you ever get bored as you're going?" Michael asks. No one answers, so he continues. "In the corner of the bathroom, in this tiny room, is her clothes hamper. That's kind of weird, right?"

Kathy and Jenna both shrug.

"When I'm done, I walk out and find her in the kitchen. She's completely naked and asks me how I like my eggs."

"Wait, wait, wait," says Jenna. "She was still naked?"

"As a jaybird," says Michael.

"That's—" says Kathy.

"Unsanitary?" finishes Jenna.

"Well, there's that," says Kathy. "And I think, it's hard to take a naked person seriously. Mark Twain said something about that."

"True, but what about the splatter? You did say she was frying eggs, right?" Jenna asks.

"Seriously, I mean, that's weird, right?" Michael asks.

His friends nod.

"I was so dumbfounded that I didn't even have time to ogle her. But I definitely was staring. I think I even said something like, over hard."

"Over hard?" asks Jenna, groaning.

"His eggs," says Kathy.

"Yes. My egg preference," says Michael. "And I don't even like 'em that way."

"Wait," Kathy says, "when did you get dressed? Weren't you naked, too?"

"Ooh, good point!" Jenna says. "Total double standard."

"First," Michael turns to Jenna, "I wasn't cooking. And second," he turns to Kathy, "I got dressed when I left the bathroom and before I came into the kitchen."

"Oh okay," Kathy says. "I'll let it slide this time."

"But details matter," says Jenna.

"Frankly, sometimes there's too many details," says Kathy, laughing.

"May I continue?" Michael asks, shaking his head.

Charlie looks concerned. "You okay? You either really like something that you see, or you're stuck in time."

"Aren't you worried about, you know, grease splatter?"

Charlie starts to laugh but stops when she realizes Michael is serious. "I am cooking you breakfast. We had a good night. So, I'm naked. I thought guys got off on that kind of thing. Don't they? Don't you?"

"Now, I knew I was going to regret this. But I stood there a moment too long, and then I had to say something. My mental-filter was down. I was tired. My nerves were frazzled. So, I just said what I was honestly thinking."

"Honesty this early in the relationship? Tsk. Tsk," says Kathy. "Now there's a novel idea."

"Hey!" says Michael "You lezbos are all about moving in after the first date. Us breeders, we like to ease into the reality of the situation. If you get my drift. Jenna, back me up here."

Kathy kicks Michael under the table.

"No," says Kathy, shaking her head.

"No," says Jenna. "Michael, ease up on the stereotyping of lesbians, it's not cool and you know better."

Michael nods and looks apologetic. "Sorry," he says. "I do know better and that was shitty of me."

"You're on notice," says Kathy, but smiles at him.

"I mean," says Jenna. "I often send my representative to the first couple dates. Sometimes even the first couple months."

"What do you mean by your, representative?" asks

Kathy.

"You know, the version of you that you think will best represent you to the potential date," says Jenna.

"Uh huh," says Kathy. "And now we might know why you've gone on one hundred dates and haven't found true love."

"What's that mean?" asks Jenna.

"It means," Kathy says. "You have to be yourself and be open in order to find someone that will accept you. The formula is supposed to help cut through the walls people put up."

"I know, I know," says Jenna. "The Love Formula is supposed to cut through the bullshit. I'm not saying it's right, I'm not saying I always do it. I'm just saying, I kind of know what Michael's talking about."

"Thank you for that," says Michael. "Anyway, so I told Charlie that it would make me a lot more comfortable if she had clothing on while she was cooking."

Charlie's mouth is agape and her eyes are wide open, staring at Michael.

"You know, for your own safety."

Charlie continues to stare at him. Her mouth closes.

"So you don't, burn yourself. You know." Michael flinches, imagining being burned by grease. "Seriously, I'm just concerned."

Charlie's eyes narrow. "What's wrong with your girlfriend making your breakfast, in the buff? Is there something wrong with the way I look? Are my love handles too big for you? You didn't seem to mind last night."

Michael looks around as if trying to find an exit.

"You have some balls," Charlie says. "I think it's best you go."

Michael sighs. "I don't do well with confrontation. I like having time to think things through. When I'm pushed, when I don't have time to sort things out and to anticipate replies, I say things that I probably shouldn't. I really didn't know what to say. I wasn't sure how she'd react to whatever might come out of my mouth. I started to consider different possible responses, and with each second of silence the pressure to say something built up and built up. But my dad always said to end with a joke."

"No, you didn't," says Jenna.

"Please say you didn't," says Kathy.

"So, a baby Harp Seal walked into a club," Michael says.

Charlie points to the door, seething with anger.

Michael stands tentatively, unsure of what to do. He begins to say something and stammers and then is silent again.

Charlie points repeatedly at the door.

Michael runs for it. Opens the door, exits, and closes the door quickly.

"Only, I had this nagging feeling that I hadn't closed the door. Fully."

Michael inspects the door to see if any light is coming in from any openings. Light pours through a crack between the door and the frame.

"It seemed closed, but I had to make sure."

Michael winces, opens the door quickly, and closes it again. He again inspects the door to see if it is really closed. The light taunts him, pouring through the crack between the door and the frame.

"It was definitely closed this time. I was sure. So sure. Still, there was that light coming through a crack in the frame. I had to make sure."

Michael is visibly sweating. He winces and opens the door again. This time Charlie catches the door as it opens.

"What the fuck are you doing?" she yells. "Are you jacking off my door?" Her face is red from anger and crying.

"Uhm, I couldn't tell if it was closed?" Michael asks.

"Here, I'll fucking close it for you." Charlie slams the door. The frame rattles, the lock turns, and Michael looks at his shoes.

"I was pretty sure it was closed that time."

"Man, you really know how to burn a bridge, don't you?" asks Jenna.

"I guess so," says Michael. "It sucks, I really liked her." Michael sighs deeply and closes his eyes, trying to hold back tears.

The three friends look at their empty mugs.

"Do you think I should call her?" asks Michael.

"No," says Jenna. "No way. No way."

"Give her a week. At least. Maybe more. If you call her now, she might come at you with an axe," says Kathy.

Suddenly Conrad's voice can be heard from down below.

"HOLY SHIT," Conrad yells. "A massive earthquake just rocked Japan!"

"What?" several voices in the coffee shop ask.

"They're saying a tidal wave is coming next, it's going to be huge," Conrad responds to anyone listening.

"Jesus," Jenna says.

"How big?" Michael yells.

"I think they said 9.0 or 9.1," Conrad responds.

"Nine?" Michael repeats, and then turns to his friends, "wait, that's really high, right?"

Conrad is either ignoring Michael's response or can't hear him.

"Yes," Kathy says. "Unheard of."

"That is," says Jenna. "Wow. Remember that one in Indonesia a few years ago?"

"That tsunami that followed was devastating," Kathy says.

The three sit in silence again. Michael finishes his mug of coffee and spins it slowly in a cupped hand.

"So, one can only assume you're doing better with your others?" Michael asks.

Kathy and Jenna look at him.

"Yeah," says Jenna. "But let's walk and talk."

"I agree," says Kathy. "I need to move and do something to clear my head. I can't even imagine what's going on in Japan right now. Not really focused on relationships."

The three rise and head down the stairs towards the door.

"Any cravings? I could go for a Blimpy burger," says Michael. "A quint will solve all woool!"

"Five patties?" asks Jenna.

"What? Look, Kathy has that hot dog place," Michael says.

"They're red hots," Kathy corrects.

"Okay, red hots," says Michael. "And Jenna has her Jerusalem Garden. Blimpy's my safe place. That's the place I go when I need some comfort."

Kathy and Jenna shrug and the three friends leave Tree Town and head down State Street.

LUNCH AT BLIMPY'S

The sidewalks are full of University of Michigan students and employees out for lunch. The trio walks toward Blimpy Burgers and talks along the way.

"If by 'comfort' you mean clogged arteries leading to death, then yes," says Jenna.

"Go easy," Kathy says. "He's clearly hurting here. Right, Mikey?"

"Right, right," says Michael. "So does that mean you're buying?"

"Let's not go that far," says Kathy. "So Jenna, what's up with you and Art-boy?"

"It's great," says Jenna. "Really, as far as I can tell, he's perfect. Opens doors for me, he can cook, he loves art, he—"

"I'm waiting for the but," says Michael. "Where is it?"

"I think I see it coming," says Kathy.

"Very funny, *but*," Jenna puts extra emphasis on the word, "you know, he's only a ninety-three percent match. I can't help but wonder if he's this great, how much better a hundred percent match would be."

"Oh boy, again with the numbers," says Kathy.

"Hush! Don't let our customers hear that," says Michael. "It is how we earn our living after all."

"Right," says Kathy. "But seriously, what's wrong with a ninety-three. That's an A right?"

"Borderline A," says Jenna. "Depending on the scale. A ninety-five is a solid A."

Kathy stops walking and looks at her friend.

"Hey, you asked," Jenna says.

"Kathy's got a point though," says Michael. "What are you going to get for an additional seven percent that you're not getting now? Maybe his socks will always land in the hamper? I mean, what exactly are we talking about?"

"Right," says Kathy. "What are David's faults?"
"I haven't found any. Yet," says Jenna. "I know, I know. But, remember Rowan?"

Kathy and Michael groan in unison.

Rowan (25) stands against the charcoal gray colored wall for you to examine. His red hair is messy, but stylish. He wears blue jeans and a plain black t-shirt. His blue eyes sparkle.

"What? That was my low point! That was what brought us to the bar in the first place. The night the Formula was born. Don't shun our past."

"Yes, yes, we know," says Kathy. "And believe me, we appreciate it. Dearly. But that poor man, his soul needs to be laid to rest."

"Seriously, every time there's a glimmer of doubt in a relationship," says Michael, "suddenly it's 'remember Rowan?' That poor guy. And now, here's David, and he doesn't even have any faults bringing you to that point, you're just anticipating that there is something. Of course there will be something, no one is perfect. Hell, sometimes I even get angry at myself. How can I expect anyone else to be any better?"

Kathy nods. "That guy was cute though, very Irish. Knew Gaelic for Christ's sake. He was good for you, I'll say that."

"I know, and David reminds me of him."

Back to that little gray room. Rowan and David stand next to each other, looking one another up and down.

Michael gestures right and left with each contrasting attribute that he illustrates. "Red hair, dark hair. Blue eyes, hazel. Hipster, athletic. Tall, average height. Irish, Italian. Yeah, I see the similarities. Practically the same person."

"They do both have great smiles," says Kathy.

"Ahh, there you go," says Michael.

"You're not helping, either one of you," says Jenna. I can't help it. I felt like I wasted five years with him, and now, you know, I'm not getting any younger."

"Right, you're practically an old maid," says Kathy. "Wasting away."

"You know, there's been talk about a quarter-life crisis," says Michael. "The new mid-life crisis. Maybe you should just buy a convertible? Or wait, what's the equivalent for women?"

Kathy rolls her eyes and Jenna sighs.

"Look," Jenna says. "We were a good match, even before I had the Formula to tell me so. He moved in with me. We were good fiscally. We shared accounts, we did bills together. We were saving for our future. We were good in bed. We traveled. We went to nice restaurants. Hell, he even bought me my favorite painting that hangs in my apartment. But I kept having that nagging feeling that he wasn't it. I stuck it out, because I couldn't place my finger on whatever it was that was missing. I felt like I owed it to him. And I didn't know what love was. So I told him. It was the hardest thing I ever did. I felt horrible. I tried to give him the Miro back. I don't even know how much he paid for it. But he was too nice. Or too hurt. Or didn't want the memory of this whole thing haunting him on the wall."

Kathy puts her arm around Jenna. "I know that was rough for you. We were there, remember? But you have to take a chance, girl. That's part of the fun."

"If by fun you mean, risk having your heart broken and stomped all over," says Michael. He laughs. "But she's right. We love you, but we're going to push you out of the nest."

"How do you know though? I mean, how do you know?" asks Jenna.

"You just do," says Kathy. "Or maybe you never do. Look at me. How many partners have I had? And yet, I keep getting up and trying again. It's trial and error. You put yourself out there and you see what happens."

Michael nods at Kathy. "And, she inspired me. I haven't even looked at the post-kiss numbers. And I'm not going to. Not that it matters, because you know, Charlie hates me and all."

The trio walks into Blimpy Burgers. A line backs up almost to the door, but it moves fast. As Michael, Kathy, and Jenna advance through the line, new people come and replace them keeping the line about the same length at all times. A sign on the wall spells out the rules for ordering. It reads:

How to order.
1. Everyone eating should get in line and order for themselves. Please do not switch places after ordering. DO NOT rush us or skip steps.
2. Grab a tray if you are eating in, otherwise we will pack your order to-go. Everyone should have their own tray (think of it like a plate).

3. Please no cell phones in line, we need your attention.

Order of operations:
1. The deep fryer. This is where we will ask you what you want from the fryer—French fries, onion rings, veggies, chili cheese fries. This is also where you can order soup and chili.
2. The Grill. This is where you order your burger (if you are ordering a sandwich, do that now, too). FIRST WE WANT: # of patties (double, triple, quad, quint, +), your bun (regular, kaiser, pumpernickel, onion), grilled items (onions, mushrooms, bacon, salami, egg, mild banana peppers). NEXT, when your meat is done, we will ask for your cheese (American, cheddar, Swiss, provolone, beau, feta, or pepper jack).
3. Dress Yer Burger. Here we will put all the cold stuff and condiments on your burger. WET STUFF FIRST: mayo, ketchup, mustard (yellow, Dijon, or stoneground). THE FREE STUFF: raw onions, dill pickles, sweet relish, and romaine lettuce). THE EXTRAS: tomatoes, banana peppers, jalapenos, black or green olives
4. Enjoy. Choose one of our specialty beverages or pick up a dessert to round out your meal. Enjoy one of the best burgers you've ever had and we will see you again soon.

Now, you might be thinking, "hey, this sounds just like the Soup Nazi guy from *Seinfeld*." And, yes, they certainly share some similarities. But the Soup Nazi—who first appeared in Episode 6, Season 7—was based on Ali "Al" Yeganeh, an Iranian American soup vendor who ran Soup

Kitchen International in New York City. The actual Soup Kitchen opened in 1984 and the episode aired in 1995. If you're a Nora Ephron fan, you might also remember a side character in *Sleepless in Seattle* (1993) pitches a story about a guy who makes great soup but is the meanest man in America. This is likely the earliest reference to the man who would achieve greater fame through *Seinfeld*.

However, this is Krazy Jim's Blimpy Burger. It's a staple of Ann Arbor and it predates Yeganeh, The Soup Kitchen, and certainly *Seinfeld*'s Soup Nazi. Who's Krazy Jim? Why it's Jim Shafer, the guy who started this place in 1953. The other half of Blimpy's fame, is Rich Magner who started working there as a student in 1969, only to return in 1993 to buy the business from his former boss. There is debate about who coined the phrase, "cheaper than food" that adorns the wall, menus, t-shirts, and all Blimpy-branded material, and a good, strong case could be made for either Jim or Rich. To work at Blimpy, you have to have character and keep the line moving. There's an attitude that everyone has that works there, and it's part of the charm.

It's not quite the Soup Nazi—then again, Yeganeh wasn't quite the Soup Nazi either—but the cooks at Blimpy's can get grumpy when the instructions aren't followed. Fortunately, this group of friends are familiar with the process and before long they're sitting at a table enjoying fried food and delicious burgers.

"Remember the first time we came here?" asks Michael.

Kathy groans, but Jenna laughs.

"Kathy, it's okay," says Michael. "Everyone has a story like that, though, maybe not quite as good as yours."

"Yes, yes, I know," says Kathy. "Make fun of the newbie, who says 'I just want cheese,' and gets, literally only cheese."

Michael laughs. "It's still funny. I'm sorry. The cooks

here really need to do stand-up or something. I wonder if that's part of the interview process."

"In fairness," says Jenna. "They really are just trying to deliver exactly what the customer asks for, without judgment. If you went to McDonald's and asked for lettuce on a bun, they'd make you repeat that five times and sign a waiver, but at Blimpy's, they just give you what you want."

"They had to know what I meant," says Kathy. "Being a server is about understanding your customer."

"That's where they got you though," says Michael. "They're not servers. They're cooks. You tell them how you want it, and they do their best to deliver it as requested."

"He's right. There are no servers at Blimpy's," says Jenna, nodding to Michael. "Just cooks and a cashier."

"So, what are we then?" asks Kathy, chewing on a fry. When no one answers, she elaborates, "with The Love Formula, are we cooks or servers?"

Michael and Jenna answer simultaneously in direct opposition to one another.

Michael glares at Jenna. "We are so obviously cooks. We prepare the menu, you figure out how you're going to interact with it, and which services you're going to use."

Jenna shakes her head. "I don't know how you can seriously say that. We literally provide a ser-vice," she breaks the word into syllables and annunciates slowly," so obviously, we're ser-vers. Customers have a need, and we serve that need. It's right there. Serve. Therefore, we are servers."

Jenna and Michael look to Kathy to break the tie.

"I'm declaring Switzerland here," she says. "You both make a strong case, and, I think you're both partially right. We do," she nods to Michael, "curate a service, or menu, and leave it up to the customer to figure out how to interact with the results we provide. But--" she nods to Jenna "-- that service is a curated one, which means we try to anticipate the needs of our customers and to provide for those needs. We are cooks and servers."

Jenna rolls her eyes and Michael grunts.

"Just like I'd argue Blimpy's should," says Kathy. "I'm sorry, I'd like to let this go, but I still don't see a world in which someone, in a burger joint, says they just want cheese and the person who is frying their patty and browning their bun doesn't give the customer a burger, with cheese, on a bun, and no other toppings!"

"I mean," says Jenna, "their rules of engagement are right on the wall. Step two is the grill and cheese phase. Step three is toppings. Cheese is not a topping."

Michael is nodding along and then abruptly stops, "What? Cheese is not a topping? Of course it's a topping!"

"When you order a pizza, do you have to say you want cheese on it?" asks Jenna.

"No, but—" Michael begins, but is interrupted.

"Right, because it's not a topping," says Jenna.

"I mean, you can order extra cheese," says Michael.

"Which implies the presence of cheese to begin with," says Kathy. "I don't really like where this conversation is going, but I have to agree with her logic."

"So, logically," says Jenna. "If you're ordering a cheeseburger, which you were, since it's implied in Step 2two we'll ask for your cheese (American, cheddar, Swiss, provolone, beau, feta, or pepper jack). They don't indicate none as an option. So, the default is a cheeseburger, just like cheese pizza is the default, unless you specify otherwise."

"If it's the default, then why do you even have to mention it?" asks Michael.

"It's about specificity and precision of language," says Jenna.

"I feel like this is all one huge smokescreen to keep us from discussing what really matters," says Michael.

"And that is?" asks Jenna.

Kathy rolls her eyes. "Letting Rowan go, embracing happiness, and moving on with your life."

"Focusing on the ninety-three, instead of the seven percent," says Michael.

"I mean, 93% is way more than half full, right?" asks Kathy.

Jenna pushes a fry around in her ketchup and looks doubtful.

ALL IN

When Kathy walked into Tree Town this morning, the first thing she noticed was Conrad was not behind the counter. He'd become a fixture and, until now, she hadn't realized how much she counted on him being there. She walks to the counter. No one is standing there to take her order.

"Hello?" she asks.

She hears a voice say, "Just a second."

Kathy considers the board of specials. It has not been updated since yesterday. She hears footsteps approaching and sees Cosmo (31).

Cosmo is dressed in tight-fitting lavender pants, white tennis shoes, a white dress shirt, blue vest, and a striped tie. He also wears a nametag.

"Sorry about that," says Cosmo. "I'm the only one here today, and I needed to run something up to two. What can I get you?"

"No apron?" asks Kathy.

"Excuse me?"

"You're not wearing an apron," says Jenna. "Aren't you nervous you'll spill? Or splash?"

Cosmo smiles, "I've been making espressos and all this for years. I'm good. No mess. Plus, this shirt is fresh pressed and fabulous."

"Doesn't Conrad want you wearing the brand?" asks Kathy.

"Conrad said he didn't care," says Cosmo. "Besides, the minute you walk into this place, you see the brand. The sign outside tells you Tree Town Coffee, the tree here reminds you of that, and everything inside has Tree Town on it. I don't think my apron will change your opinion one way or another."

"Good point," says Kathy. "I think I like you."

"Excellent," says Cosmo. "What can I get you to drink?"

"The usual," says Kathy.

"Yeah, I don't know what that is," says Cosmo. "Sorry."

"Oh, right. Okay, how about a dark roast with room for cream."

"Coming right up," says Cosmo.

"Where is the boss?" asks Kathy.

"He's up on two."

"Sitting in his own coffee shop?"

"Yep, even drinking his own coffee."

"That is--" Kathy struggles for the word-- "Unusual. Do you know if Jenna or Michael are here?"

"It's possible," says Cosmo. "There are a number of other people here, and several more forming a line behind you. But I didn't get their names."

Kathy looks behind her. None of them are Jenna or Kathy. She strains to see who's on two but can't see from her angle.

Cosmo sets a mug of coffee on the counter in front of her, and Kathy pays.

"Thank you," she says and walks towards the stairs.

Jenna and Michael aren't on two either. But she sees Conrad sitting with Grover (22) at a table. She debates about approaching, assuming they're probably working things out. At least, Kathy hopes they're working things out. She tries to appear casual and not stare but can't resist watching them. They're laughing. Grover reaches across the table and brushes Conrad's arm. Eventually, Kathy can't resist any longer. She walks over to them.

"Hey," she says.

Conrad eyes her and nods.

Grover smiles. "Hi, Kathy. Saw your friend on TV a while ago—sorry it's been so long—she looked good. It was a good interview."

"Thanks," says Kathy. "And I'm sorry I didn't chase you down for your number before you left. I always liked you and wanted to stay in touch."

"No problem," says Grover.

"So," Kathy gestures at the space between Grover and Conrad. "This? Is it happening?"

Conrad shrugs. "We're trying to work things out, but you, being here, isn't exactly helping. We were kind of in the middle of things."

"At your coffee shop?" asks Kathy. "This is where you have a serious conversation?"

"Thank you," says Grover. "I mean, whatever, right? But I thought these kinds of conversations happened in neutral territory or at the house of the person who's been wronged."

"You were wronged?" asks Conrad. "And this is neutral territory."

"This is most definitely not neutral territory," says Kathy. "It is literally your space. You own it. This is your territory. I'm with her," Kathy gestures at Grover with her mug. "You should be meeting somewhere neutral, or at her place."

"How do you know she's the one that's been wronged?" asks Conrad.

Kathy rolls her eyes. "Please."

"Right," says Conrad. "I know, I'm an idiot. But I can change. And I've been trying to do just that."

"He did get a mustache," says Kathy.

"I admire the commitment to a joke," says Grover. "Except, it kind of hurts that he's willing to make a commitment like that, but not to me."

"Oof!" says Kathy.

"Not. Helping," says Conrad to Kathy.

"Look, Connie--" says Grover.

--"Please, don't call me that in front of her, or her friends," Conrad says to Grover and then turns and scowls at Kathy.

"I'm sorry," says Kathy. "I shouldn't have butted in. I just wanted to say hi and good job on the new guy."

"Thanks," says Conrad. "I hired the new guy—"

"—Cosmo—" fills in Grover.

"Right, Cosmo," continues Conrad, "So I wouldn't have to be here all the time. So I can go places with Grover, and spend time together at a place, neutral or otherwise, that isn't the coffee shop. Because, believe it or not, I actually like doing things other than spending my life in a coffee shop."

"Be honest," says Grover. "You also hired Cosmo so you didn't have to worry about accidentally hitting on him."

"But he is kind of hot," says Kathy. "I mean, objectively."

"Are you suggesting we objectify Tree Town Coffee employees? You of all people?" Conrad smiles at Kathy.

Grover ignores Conrad and responds to Kathy's

comment. "Totally hot," nods Grover. "But not his," she gestures at Conrad with her chin, "type."

"Cosmo is hot?" asks Conrad.

Kathy nods.

Grover shakes her head. "See? No clue."

"What?" says Conrad. "It's just the way I'm wired."

"But you should be able to acknowledge beauty, regardless of attraction," says Grover.

"And style," says Kathy. "Did you see what he was wearing?"

"Seriously!" says Grover. "Definitely a step up from the black t-shirts—"

"Hey!" interrupts Conrad.

"To be fair," says Kathy. "Sometimes there are names of bands on the t-shirts."

"Sure," says Grover. "Or a logo."

"Right," says Kathy.

"I am right here!" says Conrad.

"Anyway," says Kathy. "Have Jenna or Michael be here?"

"I'm not on the clock," says Conrad.

"I asked Cosmo, but he doesn't even know what my usual is yet," says Kathy.

"It is his first day," says Grover.

"Fair," says Kathy. "So, no Michael or Jenna?"

"Again," says Conrad. "Not on the clock. Plus, there is only one more floor where they could be." He shoos her away.

"Wait, before you go," Grover calls her back.

Kathy turns on her heel. "Yes?"

"I heard you have a partner," Grover says. "Louise?"

"Indeed I do," says Kathy. She pulls up and chair and sits down.

"Yes, please join us," says Conrad sarcastically and

sighs.

"How's that going?" asks Grover.

Kathy itches the top of her nose. "It's great."

"Not very convincing," says Conrad. "Even I feel that."

Kathy rolls her eyes at him.

"It is great, really," says Kathy. "It has just required some effort. But I've always known that relationships were work and they were all about honesty, transparency, and compromise."

"Yes, yes, and yes," says Grover. She turns to Conrad and says, "Take notes."

"What's that?" asks Conrad. "All I heard coming from her mouth was, I really should be going now and then the rest sounded like the adults in *Peanuts*."

"Ignore him," says Grover.

"I usually do," Kathy says. "Anyway, I know those things, and I tell my friends that, and I believe them. And I'm relieved to have finally found my person. Or at least, I think it's my person." Kathy fidgets in her seat and fiddles with a wrapper from a straw as she continues. "But I'd be lying if I said there wasn't some measure of fear about being all-in."

"Oh?" asks Conrad.

"I just mean, am I too young to decide for my partner for the rest of my life?" asks Kathy.

"You're not getting married," says Grover. "Right?"

"Right," says Kathy. "At least not yet. But it feels like it might be headed in that direction."

"Wow," says Conrad. "I never thought I'd see the day when your guard is down enough to admit you don't have it all figured out."

"We all have our doubts," says Grover. "And you never really know."

"It's like that song by Stephen Stills," Conrad says.

Grover and Kathy look blankly at him.

"'Love the One You're With'?" Conrad asks.

"He wrote that?" asks Kathy.

"Isn't that about free love or something?" asks Grover.

"Sure, you could interpret it that way," says Conrad. "But for me, the message is always more about living in the moment. Appreciating what you have. Time and life are full of surprises, and you can't predict the future."

Kathy nods along with him. "I like that."

"Me too," Grover says. She smiles at Conrad.

The three sit in silence for a moment.

"Stephen Stills, huh?" asks Kathy.

"To be fair, I only really know that song and the work he did with Crosby, Nash, and Young," says Conrad. "But, when you write a song that good, you really don't need to be known for much more."

"Hey thanks you two," says Kathy. "I know I butted in a bit, but I guess I really needed that. I hope you both can patch things up."

Grover smiles at Kathy.

"And from what I can see," says Kathy, "I think you're well on your way. I'll show myself out."

She stands, scoots the chair under the table, and waves as she walks away.

Kathy tries the third floor, but it's empty. She sits, simply enjoying the quiet, finishes her mug of coffee, sighs, and then heads downstairs and out the front door.

100% MATCH

Jenna is sitting cross-legged on her couch with her laptop on her lap. She's reading through emails from happy customers. This is one of her favorite things to do. Not only does it make her happy that the Formula is working, but she loves reading about people happily in love. And yet, when she reads these testimonials, it makes her want her 100% match all the more. The Cars "Just What I Needed" is playing in the background.

Email#1: "... we've only been together now for three months, but it feels like we've known each other forever."

Email#2: "... she fits into my life like a glove..."

Email#3: "... somehow his 86% match feels like a 100% one. I can't imagine being happier. Thank you so much for bringing us together."

The doorbell rings. Jenna sets the laptop down, walks across the floor, and answers it. By the time she opens the door, there is no one to be seen but there is a Fed-Ex box that obviously contains flowers. She retrieves the box and goes into her kitchen. She opens the box and finds a note that simply reads, "thinking about you. David." Inside the box are: ten blue irises, ten stargazer lilies, and a square, blue vase.

Jenna trims the ends off the stems on angle, like she's been taught by her mother, opens the plant food packet, and pours water and half the food contents into the vase. Immediately after arranging the flowers and placing them on her coffee table, her laptop chimes indicating a new email. She sits down, smiles at the flowers, and opens the email. It's one of the automated notifications from The Love Formula, indicating that she has a match. She logs into the site and sees that it's a 100% match. Even though she set the alert threshold to 100% and knew that was the only way she'd receive such a notification, she has to see it for herself. She looks at the flowers and then back at the laptop.

Kathy's apartment is decked out in antiques. All the furniture is dark, heavy, solid wood, and the walls are painted bold vivid colors that contrast against the dark woods. The living room is navy blue, the bedroom is deep red, the bathroom is grass green. Black and white photographs hang from the walls. It appears as if her apartment comes from a different age and, true to form, she has no television.

Kathy has several outfits laid out on her bed. Her cell phone buzzes on the dresser. She looks at it but decided to ignore it. Her home phone rings. Kathy sighs and walks over to the phone.

"Hello?"

"I got one! I got one!" Jenna is practically screaming.

"What? Quieter, you're going to deafen me. What did

you get?”

"A one hundred percent! His name is Oscar!”

"I thought you were dating David?” asks Kathy.

"I was… I am.”

"Okay. But?”

She can hear Jenna sighing into the phone, clearly ready to confess something she's not proud of. "I adjusted my auto-search notifier so that it would only tell me about hundred percent matches. Just in case.”

Kathy eyes the outfits on the bed and seems to be favoring the one with the dark blue blouse. "Uh huh.”

"And now! I got one!”

"Sure, sure,” Kathy pairs a scarf with the blouse and considers it. "That's great. I'm really happy for you. But what are you going to do with it?” She begins pacing alongside her bed.

"I'm going to go on a date with him. I need to know.”

"Kathy stops pacing and is simply quiet.

"What?” Jenna asks. "You wouldn't do the same.”

"What do you think?” asks Kathy. "I mean, I don't think I would. Why ruin what you have?’

"But, it could be better!”

"How? What's missing now?”

Jenna is silent.

Kathy looks at the blouse and scarf and decides this is the one. "Well, good luck. I need to go. I have a date with Louise. And I still don't even know what our percentage is.” She pauses. "What's more, I don't care. But, Jenna?”

"Yeah?”

"I am happy for you. I know how bad you've wanted this. Just remember, they are just numbers. Probabilities. You make your happiness.”

"Oh boy, that sounds like something you'd see on a poster along with a kitten reminding you to hang in there.”

Kathy shrugs, even though Jenna can't see it. "Doesn't make it any less true. What are you going to do about David?"

"I don't know."

"Okay, well, have fun."

"Kathy?" asks Jenna.

"Yes?"

"I'm happy for you, too. Louise is great. I'm so happy you found someone that works for you. Have fun tonight."

"Thanks," Kathy says. "I will."

She hangs up, smiles at the outfit she's selected, and gets ready for her date.

THE STATE THEATRE

First, is "State Theatre" a typo? Should it be "er" or "re"? And what's the difference? Ask enough people, and you'll get a variety of explanations. Most say, "theatre" is British and "theater" is American. Others use "theatre" to sound classy and to indicate "high art" events (whether film or live). However, some will say, "theatre" is where live dramatic performances occur, and "theater" is for cinema. However, I have yet to really find a satisfactory source that delineates which is which. It does so happen that there are two classic theater/theatres in town. The Michigan Theater is where live performances occur, and the State Theatre is where you go to see films. To complicate matters, the Michigan Theater does sometimes show films. Of the two classic theatres in town, which are mere feet away (287 feet to be almost precise), the Michigan is the oldest and it's located on Liberty Street. It's the place you're more likely to see a concert, whereas the State is where you'd go to see a film, and it's, cleverly, located on State Street. The Michigan Theater (notice the "er" ending) was built in 1927, whereas the State Theatre ("re") didn't come along until 1942.

Since our story features a moment in the State Theatre, I'm going to focus on that one exclusively. It was built by C. Howard Crane, the same person who designed the Fox Theatre (note the "re"). The State has come in and out of vogue, and even at one time was gutted and turned into a retail space. Well, the bottom two screening rooms anyway. Urban Outfitters set up shop there, and in the early 90s, the screens came back to life. Since then, it's been updated in 1999, 2007, and 2013, then was shutdown until 2017 while they performed major renovations.

When it came back in 2017, this place was majestic and beautiful—maintaining the old Art Deco look, while updating all the projectors and accommodations within. Our story takes place from 2010-2012 though, so this is before all that. (Sorry.)

No worries though, Oscar and Jenna have a great time without the knowledge that the theatre would be shut down and renovated in the near future.

There were a number of films showing at the State Theatre in 2011. Depending on when they went, they could have seen:

Midnight in Paris—you know, the Woody Allen movie where Owen Wilson gets picked up by some of his literary heroes from the 1920s and goes on a fever-dream-like adventure with them? It was in the running, but ultimately Jenna said she wasn't a huge fan of Woody Allen movies.

Everything Must Go—Will Farrell starred in this one, and it was based on Raymond Carver's 1978 short story, "Why Don't You Dance?" Oscar was contemplating this one, because he loved Carver's writing.

Beginners—had Ewan McGregor and Christopher Plummer in it, which was a big plus. However, Oscar wasn't sure how he felt about taking his date to a movie about a 75-year-old man's coming out story.

Tree of Life—unfortunately, Oscar led with the cast, thinking that Brad Pitt and Sean Penn would entice Jenna, but she believed both actors were overblown. Had he explained the plot or artistry involved in the telling of the story, she would have been able to overcome her misgivings about the two most popular male cast members.

Terri—Oscar pled that he had heard this one was better than the reviews, but Jenna said she couldn't take John C. Reilly seriously. That was a shame.

Snow Flower and the Secret Fan—Jenna loved historical dramas, but Oscar wasn't a fan. So they passed without really even getting into the nuances of what the film was about.

Cedar Rapids—Oscar was so excited that this film had been finally made, since he heard it was one of the most popular unproduced screenplays of all time, but Jenna was convinced there was probably a reason it was unproduced.

The King's Speech—it's petty to admit, but even though Jenna loves historical dramas, she passed on this one because Oscar had passed on *Snow Flower and the Secret Fan*. Jenna did go in secret to see it on her own and was delighted when it received 12 Oscar nominations and ultimately won 4.

Potiche—Jenna eagerly wanted to see this one, primarily because of Gérard Depardieu, but Oscar said he wasn't in the mood for subtitles.

And that's to say nothing of re-runs that the State regularly ran, like, Pee Wee's Big Adventure or *Back to the Future*.

So, what did they actually see then? They saw a movie called: *Win Win*. In part, it was about timing. They had put off their date a number of times, ostensibly because they couldn't agree on a film. It was also possible that Jenna was also delaying because she was anxious to meet her 100% match, but she did a good job of coming up with excuses about why she didn't want to see this movie or that movie. Finally, after several delays, they found themselves settling on this one. They were both hit or miss on Paul Giamatti films. Jenna wasn't a fan of *Sideways*, but Oscar was. Jenna loved *American Splendor*, *The Illusionist* and *Man on the Moon*, while Oscar preferred *Cinderella Man*, *Last Station*, and *Barney's Version*. Neither of them are fans of sports movies, but Oscar argued this wasn't really about the sports. Ultimately, the deciding factor was that they both loved Bobby Cannavale, particularly for his reoccurring role on *Will & Grace*.

Win Win it was, and it was indeed a win-win. We'll pick up the story as they exit the film now.

OSCAR

A small crowd of people exit the State Theater and diverge in different directions down State Street and Liberty Street. After a beat, Jenna and Oscar (23) exit holding hands. They cross the street and head towards Red Hawk Bar and Grill.

"It's kind of funny, but despite living here all my life, I don't think I've ever been to the State Theater before," Jenna says.

"What?" Seriously? So, this was, uh, your first time?"

Oscar looks to Jenna who nods at him.

"Wow, I go all the time. Stick with me, kid, I'll show you a few things about your town."

"I could stand to learn something about independent films."

"Plus, it's just a gorgeous old theater."

Jenna scrunches up her face at Oscar. "Did you just say, gorgeous old theater?"

"I think," Oscar says, hesitating. "I think I did. Why, is that offensive or politically incorrect?"

Jenna laughs. "No, not exactly. But who says that?"

Oscar raises hie eyebrow and tentatively points at

himself. "Does that mean our date is over?"

Jenna thinks it over for a beat. "I think I'll let you slide this once, but don't let it happen again."

Oscar mimes wiping his brow.

"Alright," Jenna says. "Safer territory here: how long have you been living here?"

Oscar counts on his fingers and says, "Four."

Jenna laughs. "Four? Four what? Years? Months? Decades?"

"Well, clearly," Oscar turns his head from side to side and holds one hand alongside his face and another under his chin. "Four decades is right out. I can hardly grow a beard."

"I guess it depends on how you define a beard. I mean, how many hairs do you need before it's a beard? Ten? Fifty? And I know plenty of older people who don't have beards. That can't be a true measure of age."

"Very funny," says Oscar.

They're standing in front of the Red Hawk now, and Oscar holds the door for her, then follows her inside. The restaurant is busy. The décor is fairly basic: dark wood tables and chairs, hardwood floor, with some black and white photos hanging on the walls. The hostess leads the couple to a table. Oscar pulls out a chair for Jenna, pushes it in after she's seated, and then takes a seat.

"Four years is the answer," Oscar says. "I came here a year after high school. You know, I took a year off and then decided I wanted to live in the most liberal city in the union. But couldn't afford any of those West Coast places, and the U let me in. So, Ann Arbor it was."

"What are you studying?" Jenna asks.

"You."

"Cute, cute. I meant in school. What are you studying?"

"Mass communication."

"Oh? And you hope to?" Jenna trails off and waits for Oscar to fill in the blank.

"Duh, communicate with the masses. What else?" He laughs at his own joke. "No, seriously, I want to—"

A waiter arrives with water. He smiles at the couple. "Can I get you started with some of our maize and blue chips with spicy roasted red chili salsa, or our killer nachos? Or do you need a moment?"

"The chips and salsa sound great," Jenna says before Oscar can answer.

"Coming up," the waiter says as he heads back to the kitchen.

"You were saying?" asks Jenna.

"Initially I thought I'd go into television," Oscar says, "but I've been volunteering with a nonprofit and I really like the idea of helping them with my degree. Advertising, helping with fundraising and events. Something like that."

"That sounds very noble and exciting," Jenna says. She twirls the straw in her drink. "What's the name of the organization?"

"There are two places actually," Oscar says. "The first is the breakfast at St. Andrews. I don't even know when they got started, but they've been doing a free breakfast for as long as I can remember."

"Wow," says Jenna. "Are you religious?"

"What?" asks Oscar.

"Religious?" she repeats. "Is that your church?"

"Oh," says Oscar. "I don't think we're supposed to talk about religion or politics on the first date." He laughs a little.

Jenna's not sure he's going to continue, so she asks, "What's the other nonprofit?"

"The Ark."

"The music place?" she asks.

"Yes," Oscar says. "They're a nonprofit, too. It's fun being associated them and seeing some of the behind-the-scenes stuff."

They're quiet for a moment as they look around the restaurant, watching others eat and the waitstaff weave in and out, delivering food and taking orders.

"I'm not really," says Oscar, breaking the silence.

"Not really, what?"

"Religious," he says. "I mean, I go to church now and then with my parents, but I find myself leaning more towards Eastern religions. More focused on inner peace than the dogma of an organized, outward expression of it."

Jenna nods.

"Does that sound pompous?" asks Oscar. "Sorry, I'm never sure. Not great at these conversations on a first date when something heavy comes up."

"It's fine," says Jenna. "I can't remember the last time I went to church. And really, I only asked because you were volunteering at St. Andrews."

Oscar smiles.

Their chips arrive and the conversation continues.

Later, outside Jenna's apartment.

"You know, we kind of broke all the rules for our first date," Jenna says.

"Oh? How so?"

"Well, The Love Formula strongly advises against going to a movie on the first date."

"What's wrong with movies?"

"I love movies. Don't get me wrong. I wouldn't change anything about tonight. It was great. It's just funny, that's all."

"So, why the rule?" Oscar asks.

"In general, when you go to see a movie, you sit quietly

for two hours. You don't really get to learn anything about your date. There's no talking." Jenna shrugs.

"Well, I disagree. I think a movie is a great first date for precisely those same reasons."

"Explain. We're always open to feedback."

"First, you learn a lot about the person from the type of movie he or she chooses. Which theater you go to. How they dress to go to the movies. And then the movie is a great topic for discussion afterward."

"Yes, you can learn about the person from all those things. But I'm not sure everyone puts as much thought into the theater or the type of movie they go to so, that you clearly do," Jenna says.

"But even a lack of thought is something you learn about that person. If we had gone to see," Oscar thinks for a moment. "Oh, what is showing at the big cinema? Something like, something like, uhm, oh! One of the Harry Potter movies, or Thor, or the Pirate movies. That definitely tells you something about that person."

"What does it tell you?"

Oscar looks blankly at her.

"Pretend I made the arrangements, and we went to see Harry Potter. What would you take away from that? What would you learn?"

"That you like kids' stuff. Or that you're easily swayed by mass consumerism and advertisement. Maybe that you are secretly a witch?" Oscar pauses for a moment. "Okay, so maybe that's harder to figure out than I thought."

"Apology accepted."

"But I think if you take the flip side, say I took you to a thought-provoking movie—"

Jenna interrupts, "Which you did."

Oscar smiles. "I'm glad you thought so. I love that. But even if we had gone to Midnight in Paris or Drive or The

Three of Life, those are all showing in a bigger theater. Those are thought-provoking movies that would generate conversation. And would convey to you that I'm into something more than just pop culture."

"So, it's about pretense? About putting on a good show?"

"Oh, that doesn't sound good."

"I just mean, unless you have a conversation about why you chose the movie you did, you don't really know what that person's motivations were. Maybe all the other shows were sold out. Or maybe they had already gone on enough dates to see all the other movies, and this is all that's left. Or maybe they really like the actor who happens to be in this film, which is a departure from the previous roles he or she has played."

"All fair points."

"The conversation is what's ultimately important, and that's why we decided to make the suggestion—"

"Strong suggestion."

"Yes," Jenna nods at his interjection. "Strong suggestion to avoid movies, and to focus on the conversation."

"Fair. But," says Oscar. "One thing I think you're missing, is that being comfortable in silence is also important. And a movie gives you that opportunity."

Jenna nods.

They both stand in silence, smiling at one another. After a minute, they each lean into one another and kiss. The kiss ends, they say goodnight, Oscar skips away, and Jenna, laughing, goes into her apartment.

THE DEBRIEF

Jenna bursts through the door to Tree Town Coffee.

"Whoa! Where's the fire?" Conrad asks as Jenna approaches the counter.

"Sorry! Good morning, Conrad!"

She runs up the flight of stairs and doesn't hear Conrad ask, "Coffee?" as she runs by. When she doesn't find Michael and Kathy on the second floor, she runs up the next flight of stairs. At the top of the stairs, she attempts to collect herself before approaching her friends. She takes deep breaths and walks coolly to the friends' table.

Michael looks her up and down. "Uh, huh. So, what's his name girlie?"

"Right, don't be coy with us. Out with the details. You didn't break the rules, did you?" Kathy asks.

"No! You didn't! Did you?" Michael asks.

"Sort of…" Jenna blushes.

"Please, please, please, please don't tell me you slept with him, just because he's a 100% match," Kathy rolls her eyes.

"You got a one hundred percent match?" Michael asks. "Why did you tell me?"

"Sorry, Michael," says Jenna. She turns to Kathy. "No, I did not sleep with him. All I meant was, we went to the movies."

"The movies? Really? Boy, this guy's an original. You get a hundred percent match, and he takes you to the movies? I would have thought this would have called for champagne in diamond-coated crystal," Michael says.

"That would be very impractical stemware," says Kathy.

Michael nods and accepts that.

"He is!" Jenna blurts out. "Original that is. You just haven't met him yet. Go easy on the guy."

"Mikey's just a little sensitive because he has a man-crush on David."

"Awwww, that's cute," says Jenna. "There's nothing saying that you can't go on man-dates with David. I'll share."

Michael rolls his eyes. "Name. What's his name? This Mr. Original-I'll-Take-You-To-The-Movies person."

"Oscar," says Jenna.

"Okay," says Michael. He shrugs. "I guess that works. Last name?"

"Warbler," says Jenna. "Why? Are you going to look him up?"

"No, just curious. Warbler, like the bird?" Michael asks.

"Oh shut up," says Kathy. "What, suddenly you're an ornithologist now? Give her a break."

"I've been known to watch some birds. Anyway, stop interrupting. Names are important. I require data," Michael says. "Middle name?"

"Jaiden," Jenna answers. She smiles, clearly proud of herself. After their date, she went back through and read and re-read his profile.

"Oscar Jaiden Warbler," says Kathy. "It's, unique?"

"Wait, wait, wait," says Michael. "You're going on a

date with OJ? If you ever see him with gloves, run!"

"You're a goof," says Jenna. "He's actually pretty great. A little young, but I'll take him." She holds up a finger. "Before you ask, he's twenty-three. He's studying mass communication at the U."

"Robbing the cradle, eh?" Michael laughs. "Seven years, so when you were graduating high school, he was in sixth or seventh grade? Wow, you must have a lot in common."

"Ignore him," says Kathy. "Did you have the feeling?"

Jenna turns away from Michael and makes an obvious show of only paying attention to Kathy. "I had several feelings. Which do you mean?"

"The most important one," says Kathy. "When I met Louise, I just had this immediate sense of belonging. Everything clicked. There was both the spark and the flame."

"Explain," says Jenna.

"Yes, please do," Michael adds.

"The spark is that sexual energy you feel. The flame is the thing that keeps it burning. After I met Louise, I felt both. I've felt the spark before, but this time around I also felt this desire to lounge around in sweatpants on the weekend with this woman without any judging or expectations. There were moments of silence, and they weren't uncomfortable. We didn't have to fill the air with empty words. I felt completely comfortable just being with her."

"Well, it was just one date," says Jenna. She frowns though, clearly mulling over what Kathy said.

"It's kind of weird to admit this," says Michael. "Since I'm the guy of the group and am not supposed to have feelings."

"Yes, you are the epitome of the macho, modern male," says Kathy, shaking her head.

Michael ignores her and continues. "But I had that feeling, what Kath is explaining, when I met Charlie. It just felt, right."

"Only Charlie wouldn't be relaxing wearing sweatpants, right Mikey?" Kathy laughs.

"What?" asks Jenna.

"You know, since Charlie hates clothing?" Kathy says.

"Oh sure, laugh at my pain," Michael snorts.

Kathy reaches across the table, squeezes Michael's arm, and winks at him. "You know I only kid because I love you."

"We're going on another date tonight," says Jenna. "I'll wear fire-retardant clothing, just in case of sparks or flames."

"Good idea," says Kathy. "Can't wait to hear about it."

"What about David?" Michael asks. "Does he know what's going on?"

Jenna traces the rim of Kathy's empty coffee cup with her finger. "Not yet. I want to see where this is going before I drop a bomb on him. But, so far so good. It feels pretty good."

Michael shrugs. "Fair enough, just let the guy down easy. Tell him if he needs someone to commiserate with, I'm there for him."

"You changing teams?" asks Kathy.

Michael rolls his eyes. "Geez, everything's about sex with you lesbians. Can't two guys just get together and talk? Anyway, I need to run. I've been meaning to call Charlie. Just need to get my shit together first."

"Do you have a script with various outcomes written?" asks Jenna.

"Not yet. You know, you guys laugh at me, but everyone does it. They might not write it down, but they're running through the possibilities in their minds. I just like to see it in front of me. Writing it down helps me get all the ideas out of my head. When I'm done, I hardly even look at it."

"You probably cheated at Choose Your Own Adventure books, too, didn't you?" Kathy asks.

"Everyone did. You always held your current page with one finger and flipped ahead," says Michael. "Everyone does that."

"I did," admits Jenna.

"Not me," says Kathy. "So, definitely not everyone. You guys are horrible. One is going to plot out fictitious conversations with himself and the other is going to ensure she has a relief pitcher warmed up before she pulls her start after the second inning. Why am I friends with you again?"

Jenna and Michael bat their eyes and smile weakly at Kathy. Kathy shakes her head, and then each friend gives the other a quick hug before they head down the stairs. Jenna's the last one at the door, when Conrad calls after her.

"No coffee?" he asks.

"Not today," she smiles.

"You feeling okay?"

Jenna nods and smiles. She considers the door and leaving, and then stops. Jenna looks around, sees no customers, and sidles up to the counter. "How are you and Grover doing?"

"Better," says Conrad. "Well, we're getting there."

"Yeah?" asks Jenna, she runs her fingers through her hair and picks a strand from her t-shirt.

"I mean, she's not coming back to work any time soon, if that's what you're asking," says Conrad.

"No, I'm not. Honestly, Cosmo is a huge improvement. Grover was great," she corrects herself, "is great. But she's not made to work at a coffee shop. Unless you need a greeter, or a conversationalist. But, really, not as a maker of coffee-related things."

Conrad laughs. "Yeah, she's really not great at that. I don't know why I hired her."

"Yes, you do," said Jenna. "Don't be dumb."

"You're right. I saw something—"

"Somebody," Jenna corrects.

"Somebody," Conrad nods and echoes. "Somebody that I wanted to spend time with, and it was easier to say yes to the job than it was to be brave enough to ask her out."

"Sometimes all you need is fifteen seconds of insane courage," Jenna says. She puts her hands into the pockets of her shorts and rocks back on her heels.

Conrad considers her for a moment. "The line is twenty seconds, but yeah."

Jenna eyes Conrad. "You, too? God, that was a tear-jerker."

"I am a sucker for romantic comedies," says Conrad. "And I love animals. You put them together, and holy shit, I'm going to lose it in the theater. I convinced Grover to go see it with me."

"Do you ever go to the movies alone?"

"Sure," says Conrad. "All the time. Why?"

"Me too," says Jenna. "I never used to think it was weird, until one of my dates reacted to it. Now I think about it every time I go to buy a ticket. Weird how someone can say something that sticks with you like that."

"Well, fuck that guy."

"Stan."

"Right. Fuck Stan," says Conrad. "You know, one piece of wisdom, if I might offer it."

"Just one?" asks Jenna. She smiles and laughs a little. "You're full of wisdom, and you've never asked to offer it before."

Conrad shrugs. "Yeah, well, I'm working on being less intrusive and assuming. Anyway, life is full of people who try to round your edges and file you down. Sometimes those edges need to be rounded and smoothed," he gestures at himself. "But be careful about letting them change you into something you're not. In this life, your youness is what makes you special. Don't lose that."

"How do you know when your youness is worth preserving and when it's worth changing?"

"I'd argue that it never is worth changing," says Conrad. "But the key is knowing yourself. Most of the shit that needs to change is the front, the masks we wear, the walls we've built up. None of that is really, truly you. It's just a buffer we've built to defend ourselves. Buffers serve a purpose, but you also need to know when to let your guard down and let people in."

Jenna nods. "Like with Grover?"

Conrad smiles.

"Thanks for that," says Jenna. "Have a good night, Conrad."

"Night," says Conrad.

Jenna opens the door and walks out onto the street.

SLIDING DOORS

Jenna paces in her apartment. She alternates looking at her phone and the painting on her wall. If this were a film, perhaps you'd see some quick cuts of Jenna straightening things or sitting in different positions around her apartment. And then, after just enough of that to give you the sense of impatience and procrastination, then we'd stop with the cuts and give you a long-extended scene, like what follows here.

After several false starts, she picks up the phone and dials David. He picks up after the second ring.

"I was beginning to wonder… it's been a while."

"Yeah, it has. Sorry," says Jenna.

"What's up?"

Jenna chews her bottom lip.

"Oh boy, you're probably chewing your bottom lip right now, aren't you?"

"No," Jenna says. "I'm not."

"Uh uh," says David. "I can tell something's on your mind. Just tell me." He hums the Jeopardy thinking music as he waits. "Okay, I'm coming over."

"No—"

The line goes dead. Jenna puts down the phone and stands in silence for a moment. Then races around the apartment picking up clothing and books and tries to find a place to put them.

In a movie, this could be played for laughs by running everything at double speed. Or maybe doing a split screen where you see David running down the various streets of Ann Arbor on one screen and Jenna racing around cleaning. Or maybe the cut between the dead line and the buzzer is comically and impossibly short, almost suggesting David is some kind of Flash-like superhero.

The buzzer buzzes. Jenna looks at the button on the wall near the door.

The buzzer buzzes again. She walks calmly and slowly to the wall and presses the button. Footsteps can be heard climbing the stairs. When they stop, there's a knock at the door. Jenna opens the door and David enters.

"Hey," Jenna says.

"Hey," David says.

Jenna gestures to her couch and they sit on opposite sides.

"Soooo…" David draws out the word; he's out of breath.

"Did you run here?" Jenna asks.

"Maybe?" he answers, leaning on his knees. "Okay, I'm good." He turns and looks expectantly at Jenna.

"I'm not good with these. Just hear me out. There are a lot of thoughts rattling around inside here and I need to get them out."

David nods.

"I really like you. Things have been going really well. I've been happy," Jenna says.

"Good. All good things. Good. That's good, right?"

"I got the flowers last week and I loved them."

The flowers are wilting in the square vase on the coffee table. Jenna and David both look at them.

"You should probably throw those out," he says. "I can get you new ones."

"Okay, here it is," says Jenna. "I received a one hundred percent match."

David's mouth begins to open, but he stops himself. Jenna gauges his face for reaction.

"I wasn't cheating on you," says Jenna. "I wasn't looking. I just set my filters to see what might happen. When I got one, a hundred, I just had to know. I'd never gotten one before. All day long I read about these people who are so happy with their one hundred percent matches. I really wanted to know what that was like. I had to know. I just had to. I just did. We went on one date. I need to see where it goes. I don't want to lie to you. I don't want to keep secrets. I didn't want to hurt you. I mean, I don't want to hurt you. If I hurt you. I don't know, hard to have hurt you until just now when I told you this. Unless you knew somehow, did you know somehow? I'm sorry. I said I'm bad at these things."

Jenna shifts on the couch to face David directly.

"Is that all the stuff in your head?" David asks.

"Pretty much. I guess I thought I had more," Jenna pauses. "I could come up with more, but no, that's really it."

"My turn then?" David asks.

"Sure. Yes."

"First, thank you. I do appreciate knowing. I appreciate the honesty and that you told me. But what the hell is a one hundred percent match anyway? What does it mean? It's just some computer program matching profiles and spitting out a number. What does it really mean? Is it a hundred for life? Is there some guarantee that it will continue to mean you're a one hundred percent match? Forever? Don't people change? For better and for worse, I might add. A hundred percent is just about timing. It's a perfect match, whatever that means, at this point, at this now. On paper, you and Mr. One Hundred might be perfect for one another. But real life isn't some simulation. There is no control over the variables. Shit happens. People grow. People change. Bad stuff happens to good people."

David leans forward. Jenna shifts and looks as if she's going to say something but stops herself. She looks at his shoe and then, when she finally looks back at his face, David begins again.

"We weren't a one hundred percent match, but couldn't we grow into that? Shouldn't all relationships have some room to develop and evolve? If you're one hundred percent with someone, where's the fun? Where's the room for flexibility? Plus, what if the one hundred percent is simply user error? What if someone entered their height wrong? Or if someone accidentally said their favorite color was green, when it was actually blue?"

David pauses and licks his lips. He waits to see if Jenna is going to be patient and wait, and when she does, he continues.

"One last thing. I appreciate your formula. It introduced me to you and I love it for that. I love you for creating it, and all that heart and soul you and Michael and Kathy put into it. But there are limitations to everything. You can't computerize every aspect of human nature. User profiles don't and can't possibly encapsulate everything that makes someone tick. And the minute there's something excluded, there's room for error. However minor that might be. That grain of sand in the Vaseline. It's there. I'm not saying that to put a hex on your potential relationship with a hundred percent match, it's just the truth."

Jenna looks at her lap and then slowly back up at David.

He lowers his head. "I know you've made up your mind." David shrugs.

"I just need to know. I'm sorry."

"Don't be. I had to say my piece. I had to fight for what I want. Wanted. Whatever. But I knew the minute the phone rang. I just knew." David stands, walks to the door, opens it, waves, shrugs, steps out, and closes the door behind him.

Jenna sits in silence looking at the door for a beat, then the wilting flowers, then back at the door. Her phone rings and breaks her reverie. It's Kathy.

"You and OJ down for a double date with me and Louise?"

"You don't have 'headed off a cliff' on the agenda do you?"

"What? Oh, very funny. I see what you did there. I guess I could make a crack about telling OJ to leave the glove sat home, and we'll call it even? Pick you up in ten?"

"Oscar doesn't have class, so I'm guessing he'll be game."

Jenna calls Oscar to confirm, hangs up the phone, and then takes care of the flowers. As she pulls the dead and wilted flowers from the vase, there's one iris that is still hanging on.

DOUBLE DATE

Kathy drives with Louise's hand on her knee. Oscar and Jenna sit in the back with an open seat between them. The sun is shining, and college students are all over the city. Sometimes they block traffic with their jay walking and other times they loiter outside buildings. Kathy's car navigates the streets with practiced ease.

"That wasn't necessarily the best food ever," says Louise. "But it was the perfect food for tonight. You know what I mean?"

"Yep," says Kathy.

"What was that appetizer called?" asks Oscar.

"Bruschetta," says Jenna. "I love that stuff. Especially with goat cheese. So good."

Oscar fiddles with his phone.

"Hey, Kath," says Jenna. "You got any tunes in this thing?"

Kathy scoffs. "Always."

She turns on her iPod and hits play. The Beatle's "Yellow Submarine" begins to play. Jenna, Kathy, and Louise all sing along. Oscar looks amused and smiles at them.

"Such a good song," says Jenna. "And you know, comparatively, it's one of their crappiest."

"They have so many great songs," says Louise.

"I agree," says Kathy. "What's your favorite?"

"Just one?" Louise laughs. "I'm a George fan, so I always go with 'While My Guitar Gently Weeps.' Plus, it features Clapton on that solo. God, it's an amazing song. It makes the hair on the back of my neck stand up. Every time I hear it."

"And here I thought Kathy was the only one who could do that for you," says Jenna.

Louise looks at Kathy in mock astonishment.

"Boy! You really do tell her just about everything, don't you?" Louise laughs. "What about you, Jenna? What's your favorite?"

"Difficult to say. But, with a gun to my head, let's hope that never happens, I'd probably say 'And Your Bird Can Sing.' I'm a sucker for the whole *Revolver* album."

"Oh, good one!" Louise says. "That's my favorite of their albums, too. All their others have great songs, but that one has such a beautiful cohesive feel to it. I love it. What about you, hon?"

"You mean, you don't know? Geez. It's only my ringtone for you."

"Oh, 'Norwegian Wood.' Right, I should have known that," says Louise. She smiles at Kathy.

"Yellow Submarine" ends and "I'm Looking Through You" begins. After the first couple bars, Kathy cranes her neck to see Oscar in the rearview mirror. He's still messing with his phone.

"And you, oh silent one?" she asks.

It takes Oscar a minute, and then he apologies. "Oh, sorry. Me? I don't really have a favorite."

Jenna playfully pokes him in the side. "Come on, we

love all their songs, too. But, gun to your head, you have to choose." She aims a finger gun at him.

"Uhm, probably, 'Imagine' then?"

Jenna playfully makes a buzzing sound: "Bzzzt! That's a John song. Not the Beatles. Try again."

"Oh, that one song that goes like, 'Baby, I'm amazed the way you love me' or something? You know, I can't remember the title," Oscar says.

Jenna's smile fades as she makes a weaker version of the buzzing sound made earlier. "'Maybe I'm Amazed.' Not baby. And that's Paul's work with Wings," Jenna corrects.

Kathy and Louise eye one another in the front.

Oscar shrugs and looks uncomfortable. "That, 'So This Is Christmas' song?"

Jenna sighs.

Oscar resumes fiddling with his phone, writing a text to someone. When he finishes, he notices the silence in the car. "What? I mean, I'm sorry, The Beatles were just a long time ago and there are lots of bands and music that have come since then. I'm sure I could school you on plenty of artists that are important to me that you don't know well."

"He has a point there," says Louise. "Music is very subjective and there is a lot to choose from."

"And just because he can't name a favorite Beatles song by name," Kathy adds, "doesn't mean he doesn't love their music. Or that it hasn't influenced the music he loves."

Jenna nods. "Is there any music that hasn't been influenced by The Beatles?"

In the front, Kathy and Louise both shrug.

"If something is around long enough, it's bounce to influence everything that comes after it," Oscar says. "And, really, in truth, I like music but it's not something I spend a lot of time listening to. It's nice to have something in the background and I'll go to a concert here and there, but it isn't like I always need a soundtrack to my life."

"'Soundtrack to my life'," Jenna repeats. She sighs.

The song ends as Kathy pulls the car to the curb.

"I think this is your stop, kiddos," says Kathy.

Jenna and Oscar exit the car.

"Thanks for the fun night," says Jenna. "Dinner was great. See you tomorrow morning? At the usual place?"

"Sure thing," says Kathy, smiling. "Same Bat-location, same Bat-time."

The car pulls away from the curb.

"Since we're right here, I'm going to run into the library," Oscar says. "See you later?"

"Sounds good," Jenna says.

They kiss briefly and Oscar jogs up the steps to the library doors.

PEEING IN THE SHOWER

Jenna walks through the entrance to Tree Town, lost in thought.

"Wake-up juice?" asks Conrad.

"Huh? Oh, sorry Conrad. Uhm."

"Boy trouble?"

"Something like that. Dark roast, actually, please."

Conrad pours the coffee, hands the mug to Jenna, and smiles. "You know, despite my reputation as a grump and a bad boy, I am a good listener. You know, if you need that sort of thing."

"Thanks, I appreciate that." Jenna sips her coffee. "You know, I always knew that about you. You're just a big teddy bear."

Conrad winks.

As she approaches the steps, Cosmo waves and smiles.

"Morning," Cosmo says. "You look tired."

"Yeah," says Jenna.

"You sure that dark roast is going to be strong enough?" Cosmo asks. "You know light roast has more caffeine in it, right?"

"Thanks, Cozzie, but I'm good."

"Cozzie, eh? Didn't realize we were at the nickname part of our relationship," Cosmo says, laughing.

Jenna smiles and climbs the stairs to the third floor, where she finds her friends waiting.

"Emergency, huh?" asks Kathy. "And yet, you stopped for coffee."

"Hey, I run on this stuff," says Jenna. "Go easy on me."

"What's up?" asks Michael.

"Oscar pees in the shower."

"Ewwwww! Like, on his feet?" asks Michael.

"Well, no, but, still." Jenna pauses. "I mean, actually, I guess I don't know if he pees on his feet or not. I would guess not, but now I'm rethinking everything I thought I knew."

"Can't he wait or go before?" asks Michael.

Michael and Jenna both look at Kathy, noticing she is conspicuously silent.

"Fine, I pee in the shower," Kathy says. "There, you happy?"

"What?" Michael is shocked. "I thought the female of the species was the clean one. The careful grooming cat to the masculine dog with shit stuck to its fur. Wow."

"Doesn't it run down your leg?" Jenna asks. "At least guys are equipped to..." Jenna makes a shooing gesture with her hands. "Make it go out and away."

"Look," says Kathy. "Sometimes I get in the shower and I forget to go. And sometimes the warm water—You know that trick with putting a sleeping person's hand in warm water? Let's just say it really works. Plus, I'm in the shower. It's a place to clean oneself. Right?"

"Wow," says Michael. "That's just gross." He shakes his head as if trying to erase the memory. "Anyway, you called an emergency meeting about your boyfriend pissing in the shower? There's gotta be something more. Right?"

Michael and Kathy both look at Jenna.

"Please tell me I didn't get out of my warm comfortable bed to come to the coffee shop just to learn that Oscar pisses in the shower," Michael says.

"Of course there's more," says Jenna. "We need to re-evaluate the profile of the formula. There are obviously things we're not taking into consideration."

"Like peeing in the shower?" asks Kathy.

"Yes," says Jenna.

Michael laughs. "You want a button people can click for whether or not they pee in the shower?"

"Something like that," Jenna is dead serious. "A girl's gotta know what she's getting into."

Kathy shakes her head. "Jenna, how do I put this gently? You, you really care about very specific things. Highly specific things."

"What do you mean?" Jenna asks.

Flashback to three years ago: Jenna is looking at Kathy's blouse. She says, "Hey Kathy. I love the buttons on that blouse, they look like they're almost metallic but also have an organic look to them. Cute!"

Flashback to nine weeks ago: Jenna is looking at Michael's shorts. She says, "I love how shoelaces have those little plastic wrappings at the tips. Did you know they're called aglets? They do such a good job of holding the strands together and fitting through the eyelets."

Flashback to eight days ago: Jenna is sipping coffee from a favorite mug. She says, "This mug is just perfect. A lot of mugs have an edge to their lips. This one is nicely rounded and feels pleasing on my lips. It really adds an extra element of joy to my coffee experience."

"Okay, fair enough," says Jenna. "But aren't you the person who broke up with someone because she called her vagina a frontbutt?"

Michael bursts into laughter, spraying coffee on himself and the table. "What? Oh my god, I've never heard that before." He abruptly stops laughing and adds, "And yet, you know I could totally see why someone might arrive at calling it that. Just strange to prioritize the butt and work from that as a starting point."

"That's not fair," says Kathy. "I didn't break up with her because she called it a frontbutt. I thought it was funny and she didn't like that I laughed. But the bigger deal was she couldn't bring herself to say the word: va-gin-a."

"But if I care about peeing in the shower, and you care about people being able to say vagina," Jenna says, before adding, "and Michael cares about having sheets on his bed."

"Or the ability to wear underwear," Michael interjects.

"'Or the ability to wear underwear'," Jenna echoes. "Don't you think at least some of our users will, too?"

"We can't add everything to the profile," says Michael. "It's impossible to control for everything. The form would be incredibly long. It already is. It's the biggest complaint we have about the service."

"And yet," Kathy adds. "It's the thing people love most about it, how complete it is. But I agree with Mikey, we can't build everything in. Our job is to focus on the big things and make matches based on that. At a certain point, people have to be on their own to interact, converse, and figure it out on their own."

"What about laughter?" Jenna asks.

Kathy raises her eyebrow and looks at Michael for an answer. He shrugs.

"Mary Poppins has a speech about it. Some people laugh their noses… some people laugh through their teeth… some people too fast… some can't make up their mind," says Jenna, forgetting some of the examples.

"And?" asks Michael.

"Isn't laughter an important element to include on the profile?" asks Jenna.

"You want a sliding bar from goofy to raucous with joyful in the middle?" asks Kathy. She snorts slightly.

Jenna frowns at her friend.

"I get what you're saying," says Michael. "But that's something people need to decide for themselves. That's what the date is for. Remember? The human element? That's why people come back and update the site after the date. After the kiss."

"Well, what about music then? How can I take someone seriously as a 100% match if they don't love the Beatles?" Jenna asks.

Conrad appears suddenly with a pot of coffee for refills. "Or Fugazi. I mean, talk about deal breakers."

"Who?" asks Jenna.

"Right," says Kathy. "I think our friend here has just made our point for us. We can't anticipate dealbreaker musicians for everyone. There's no universal choice. Just like laughter. I mean, goofy to you might be endearing to someone else."

"Plus," says Michael. "There's already a section of the profile for favorite musicians." He shrugs. "Where is this all coming from?"

"Favorite, sure, but what about bands I can't stand? Isn't that just as important?" asks Jenna.

"Answer Mikey's question: where is this all coming from?" asks Kathy.

Conrad takes a seat next to Michael. "It's pretty

obvious. Her boy. Am I wrong? Oh, and I did purposely use the word *boy* because he's, what? Fifteen?"

"Don't you have customers to serve?" asks Jenna.

Conrad gestures to the coffee pot and sweeps a hand over their full mugs. "I get the hint, but let me just add, I'm with Kathy. What annoys you with him is going to be the thing that clicks with someone else. Or what should drive you insane doesn't even matter because it's the right person. No computer can anticipate that."

"He pees in the shower. His laugh grates on my nerves. And the only Beatles' songs he knows are 'Imagine' and 'Maybe I'm Amazed'," says Jenna. She rolls her eyes and looks sadly at Kathy, who offers a consolatory shrug and smile.

"And?" asks Michael. "Well, obviously the pee thing is gross. I get that. But what's wrong with those songs? Too commercial for you? Need something on the b-side of the single? Obscure, Japanese-only release?"

"No!" Jenna practically screams. "Those aren't even Beatles' songs! Those are Lennon and McCartney songs!"

"Right…" Michael says. "And those guys were in the Beatles? Correct?"

Jenna growls and throws up her hands.

"Uh, no," says Conrad. "'Imagine' is John and 'Maybe I'm Amazed' is Paul."

"You're still here?" asks Michael.

Conrad sneers at him but remains standing nearby.

"Hey, at least the kid is in the right vicinity," says Michael. "Make him a mix tape. Or mix CD. Or whatever. Educate the kid. Oh, and sorry about the kid-thing, I just can't help myself."

"And you might want to cut him some slack," says Kathy. "It's not like there aren't things about you that drive him nuts. Even if he's your one hundred percent."

"God, you guys sound just like David," says Jenna. "But I do like the idea of the mix tape."

"You might have to create him a playlist and share that with him," says Michael. "I'm not sure he's ever held a cassette, or CD, in his hands."

Jenna punches Michael in the arm. "Har, har. Very. Funny."

"I agree," Conrad says. "Not that you need my approval. But education seems like the right approach here. Give him a chance. It's hard not to love the Beatles."

"What he said," Kathy says.

"And with that," Conrad says, "I'm off to the main level to make the kind of fancy drinks that keep the lights on."

"Hey!" says Jenna. "We pay for our coffee!"

"I'm just giving you a hard time," Conrad says. "But a few cold brews, lattes, and mochas go a long way to being able to pay Cosmo's paycheck." He laughs as he walks away.

"I guess, after all this," Michael says, "given everything you've said, what is it that you see in Oscar?"

"What do you mean?" Jenna asks.

"I think our friend means, and correct me if I'm wrong," Kathy says, "that you seem to have a long list of complaints about Oscar. I don't really know that you've said anything positive about him."

"Right," says Michael. "So, why are you holding on?"

"He's my one hundred percent!"

"Okay," Michael says trailing off and then adding, "but he seems like a shitty one hundred percent if you're full of complaints."

"About music, about uhm, bathroom habits, about," Kathy says and gestures "on and on" with her hands.

"By the numbers," Jenna says, "on paper though. He's one hundred percent. He's the best option out there."

Kathy and Michael shrug at her.

"But aren't we supposed to believe in our product?" Jenna asks.

"We do," says Michael.

"And we logically can," says Kathy. "Clearly, it's working. Lots of people are finding happiness."

"Two out of three owners agree," says Michael.

Jenna groans.

"Let me ask you this," Kathy says. "What do you like about Oscar? Numbers aside, what does he have going for him?"

"Well," says Jenna. "We share a lot in common."

"Art?" asks Michael.

"No."

"Music?" asks Kathy.

"Some?" Jenna says, more as a question than a statement.

"Film?" asks Michael.

"Ugh," groans Jenna. "I can't put it into words, but when we sit down and spend time together, we have good conversations. He's smart and funny."

"Those are good qualities," says Kathy. "But is it enough for you?"

Jenna remains silent.

"I can't remember who said it," Michael says. "It was probably in a documentary or on a TV show or something, but a couple was talking about being in an arranged marriage. At first, the couple didn't think they had anything in common, but they said they chose to love the person and make it work."

"Are you suggesting the Formula could be used for arranging marriages?" asks Jenna. "Because that would allow us to reach a new demographic."

Michael shakes his head.

"Jenna," Kathy says. "I think he's just saying, you have a decision to make. You go with your numbers and choose to love this person and make it work, or you go with where your heart is pulling you."

"And that's towards David?" Jenna asks.

"You tell us," Michael says.

"Why does the Formula work so well for others and just not me?" Jenna asks, burying her head in her folded arms.

"Hey," says Michael. He scooches his chair over and puts his arm around Jenna. "It's alright. I think you're just so committed to the idea of perfection that it's getting in your way."

Jenna's face is still buried, so she doesn't see Kathy nod.

"It's like me," Michael says.

Jenna raises her head and looks questioningly at him.

"I always get in my head, all worked up about things and then I'm my own worst enemy. I'm constantly tripping over myself," Michael says, sighing. "If I could just get out of my own way, then it would probably go a lot better. I'm trying to do that more."

"Mikey's right," says Kathy. "We're often our own worst enemies. Sometimes you just have to step out of the way and let life happen. Be an active participant of course, but you can't anticipate everything."

"Like every category or consideration for the formula," Michael says.

Kathy nods. "I think a lot of our customers are just using The Love Formula as a starting point. It's an opportunity to meet and match, and then they decide for themselves and trust their own judgment."

"Computers are good for many things," Michael adds, "just not everything."

"Trust your gut," Kathy says. "I mean, you managed to find some pretty awesome friends without the aid of

technology."
Michael points at Kathy and says, "What she said."

THE MIXTAPE

Jenna knocks on Oscar's door. After a few seconds, he answers. Oscar is casually dressed and obviously not expecting company.

"Oh hey, nice surprise. What's up?" he asks. He opens the door wide and invites Jenna inside.

"No, sorry, I don't have time right now. But I brought you something." She hands Oscar a CD.

"Cool," he turns it over in his hands. "Thanks. What is it?"

"A CD," she says. "Sorry, compact disc."

"Right, right, I've seen these before." He rolls his eyes. "I mean, what's on here? There's no tracklist here." He taps the plastic case that holds the CD.

"Ugh, sorry about that," Jenna says. "I totally blanked on printing the playlist. It's a Beatles mixtape. Well, it's a CD, not a tape. But you know. It's music."

"Thanks. I'll give it a listen," he says. Then frowns. "Can you send me the list of songs though? I really like to know what they're called as I'm listening."

"Sure," Jenna says. "I'll email it. They're some of my very favorite songs. Some you probably should know, or at least will sound familiar. And some that are a little edgier and less popular."

Oscar nods and smiles. "Is this because of the whole John Lennon thing the other day?"

"Sort of, maybe. Yes. Sorry," Jenna looks down. "It's important to me. This band is the foundation of so many memories and things I love." She sighs. "I really do feel terrible about how that went. I made some assumptions that I shouldn't have and overreacted."

"What kind of assumptions?" Oscar asks.

"That the Beatles are ubiquitous and that everyone loves them as much as I do," says Jenna.

Oscar laughs.

"It feels like my baseline assumption is that everyone is just like me," Jenna says. "And then the process of getting to know them is learning where and how that assumption falls short."

"I get that," Oscar says. "And you find a perfect match and assume that means you'll share everything in common."

Jenna nods.

"But that's impossible, isn't it? To share everything in common with someone?"

"Maybe a twin?" Jenna shakes her head. "Or a clone?"

Oscar laughs. "And what fun would that be?"

She sighs. "Okay, I need to run. Give it a listen."

"I will," Oscar says. He smiles and leans in for a kiss.

Jenna leans forward and pecks Oscar's cheek. He waves and closes the door.

Michael stands outside the door of Charlie's apartment. He paces back and forth and mumbles to himself. Finally, he takes a deep breath, lets it out, and knocks.

"Just a minute," Charlie says from inside.

The door opens and Charlie stands there with her arms crossed.

"I know I probably waited too long, and I made a huge ass of myself," Michael says.

Charlie raises her eyebrows and nods slowly.

"I had this whole long thing planned. In my mind. What I would say. You know."

Charlie's lips turn into a tight smile.

"Okay, here I am though. Unscripted, because I forgot it all, and because I know you can't plan for everything and sometimes you just need to wing it and let the anxiety go. Ready for unscripted Michael?"

Charlie nods and shrugs with a smile. "Let's see what you got."

"You're beautiful and I'm sorry," Michael says.

Charlie sighs, her smile softens, and she opens the door wider.

"That it?" she asks.

"I mean, I could stumble around a little more," says Michael. "But ultimately it's just a lot of sorrys and realizing I've been an idiot and behaved poorly. That I should have communicated better with you and let you inside my head instead of making assumptions and trying to protect you from the crazy," he points at his head, "up here."

"You're not crazy," Charlie says.

"I definitely have—issues?" Michael says. "I don't know the right word."

"Everyone has issues," Charlie says. "That doesn't mean we can find our way through them."

Michael nods and itches his nose.

"And, if I don't know what the landmines are, I won't know where to look and how to avoid them," Charlie says. "And you need to know about my landmines, too."

"You have landmines?"

Charlie rolls her eyes. "Clearly."

"I am really sorry, "Michael says.

Charlie smiles and says, "What took so long? Come on in."

Jenna is casually walking down East Liberty and window shopping. She pauses at Encore Records to admire their display of vintage vinyl.

Encore began life as Liberty Music Shop. A place where Peter Dale used to work in high school and through college. Peter also served in the Army, lived in Detroit, was a stay-at-home dad, and then in 1993 moved back to Ann Arbor and bought Liberty Music, renaming it Encore Recordings. Same location, 417 E Liberty St, Ann Arbor, just with a new name. At the time, there were eleven other record stores to choose from in Ann Arbor—Wazoo, Discount, Tower, Schoolkids, PJ's, and State Discount among them. What made Encore stand apart was they trafficked almost exclusively in used CDs and cassettes; things college students could afford. And, because college kids needed money, it was a handy place to offload music they weren't using. Encore didn't pay much, but they also didn't charge much. They also carefully screened what they bought, so you knew if you bought something from Encore, that you were getting quality—not some scratched-up piece of garbage that was used as a coaster. Eventually, they grew into a record, actual vinyl, behemoth. How many records did they have? At one count, they had 20,000 45s, three times as many 33 1/3rds, to say nothing of the CDs, cassettes, VHS tapes, DVDs, reel-to-reels, and wax cylinders. When Dale was ready to retire in 2011, two longtime employees, Jim Dwyer and Bill McClelland, bought it and dropped the "ing", rebranding as Encore Records. The transition was so seamless that casual shoppers like Jenna didn't even notice the change.

The door to her right opens, and David steps out into the street. He looks left first, then right, and sees— her.

She's lost in their fish-themed record display. The window display consists of albums with actual fish on the covers: *Law of the Fish* by The Radiators, *Fish Inn* by The Stalin, *Wailin' with Winnie* by Winnie Gould with Larry Fontine and his Orchestra; *Bark* by Jefferson Airplane, and *The Fourteen Bar Blues* by Bennie Wallace. But it also stretches that definition of "fish" to include *You Can't Hide Your Love Forever* by Orange Juice and *Trout Mask Replica* by Captain Beefheart and his Magic Band. And then there are albums that have "fish" in the title, but don't actually feature fish in the art: *Shaved Fish* by John Lennon and the Plastic Ono Band, and *I-Feel-Like-I'm-Fixin'-To-Die* by Country Joe & the Fish. Then, seemingly haphazardly included, are titles like: *Tattoo on my Chest* by Luke Baldwin—featuring a man with an open shirt displaying a tattoo of a jackalope on his chest; and *Broomstick Horse Cowboy* by Sharon Lowness—where Sharon is surrounded by well-loved and abused stuff animals. Jenna's trying to figure out how they fit into the rest of the display, and ultimately decides the staff includes them just to fuck with people.

Jenna notices David and asks, "Where do you think they find all this stuff?"

"I appreciate their sense of humor," says David. "I suspect they go out of their way to buy the most random things they can find."

"Can you believe that someone in the band, let alone the record company, green-lit these designs?" asks Jenna.

David laughs and then scratches the side of his face. "How goes it?"

"Oh, it goes."

"Everything you hoped for?"

"Encore Records never disappoints. I'm always impressed by their display," she nods at the wall of records in the window. "But I'm guessing that's not what you mean."

"No."

Jenna nods, she knows what he meant.

"We're still just getting to know each other," Jenna says. "How are you doing?"

David pats the bag he's holding. "I got some great vinyl here."

"Anything I'd like?" she asks.

"Maybe." David shrugs. "Anyway, good to see you." He waves and walks up the street.

Jenna stands rooted to her spot, watching him leave.

TRYING AGAIN

The sun is shining, and it is June 2011. There are a variety of news stories we could cover, perhaps by showing clips on TV or the characters walking by a newspaper stand, things like the Arab Spring continuing, New York's Marriage Equality Act, the space shuttle finishing its final mission, the PlayStation network being hacked, various sporting events and championships concluding, but none were bigger than the death of Bin Laden. Somehow, it felt a little surreal that, after all these years, it was abruptly announced. It just suddenly was, and then the world went on. Now we'd cut away from the clips or newspaper headlines and cut to the interior of Jenna's apartment.

Jenna opens the door to her apartment and finds Oscar standing there.

"Hello," she says.

"Hi," Oscar says. "Can I come in?"

Jenna seems dazed and shakes her head. "I'm sorry, yes, please."

Oscar steps inside and kisses Jenna on the way. "I really enjoyed the mixtape," he says.

"Oh?"

"Yeah, so many of those songs are ones I've heard before," says Oscar. "I mean, they're huge songs of course, everyone's heard them. But I guess I just wasn't paying close attention to them. I think when you're like the Beatles, and you're that big, you're just everywhere and then people—well, me at least—take them for granted. Sorry about that."

"I think they've done fine for themselves," says Jenna.

Oscar laughs. "I mean, obviously they're really important to you. Thanks for taking the time to put together some of your favorites for me."

"You can't really go wrong with any of their albums," says Jenna.

They stand in silence and then Jenna gestures to the couch. They find their way through the furniture and sit next to each other. Oscar sits sideways so he's looking at Jenna.

"So, what are you up to today?" asks Jenna.

Before Oscar can answer, a knock at the door interrupts.

"Grand Central Station here all of the sudden," says Jenna. She gets up and answers the door. Michael bursts into the apartment.

"Jesus, you're not going to believe this. Just when I think I know her and we're on the same page," says Michael, "all of the sudden she's talking to her mother about her vagina and I hear her say..." He sees Oscar and stops. "Oh, sorry."

"What?" asks Jenna.

"No problem," says Oscar.

"I'd say I can come back," says Michael, "but I really need the brain trust here and Kathy is busy," he looks at Jenna and Oscar. "But maybe you're busy, too?"

"No, not at all," says Oscar. "It's okay." Oscar looks at

Jenna. "Right?"

"Sure, I guess?" replies Jenna. "Do you mind standing in for Kathy?"

Oscar shrugs. "Not at all. I guess it's kind of an honor, right?"

"Okay, great," says Michael.

Jenna takes her seat on the couch next to Oscar and they both watch Michael as he paces back and forth in front of them.

"So, Oscar some of this you'll just have to get caught up on or figure out or whatever, like Charlie doesn't like to wear clothes, but whatever. Anyway, we're doing our thing, and then her phone rings. So, she goes to answer the phone." Michael paces and mimes being Charlie on the phone. "She's all talking in the kitchen to her mom and all of a sudden I hear her say the word: vagina." Michael stops for a reaction.

Oscar raises an eyebrow and turns to look at Jenna.

"Okay?" says Jenna. "I mean, people use lots of different words in conversation, and vagina is just another word. An anatomical word."

"A biological word," Oscar adds.

"But to her mother?" asks Michael. "I mean, Oscar, I don't know about you, but I don't often say 'penis' to my dad. Do you?"

Oscar fidgets and then shrugs. "No."

Before he can elaborate, Michael continues. "Exactly. You just don't talk about genitalia with your parents."

"That's not what I said," says Oscar.

Michael ignores him. "So, I come out of the bedroom and watch her walking around the kitchen, picking up things and talking to her. She finishes and hangs up. And I ask her, what was that all about? She seems completely surprised that I wonder why my girlfriend is talking about her vagina to her mother."

"I mean," says Jenna. "It is her mother. It's not like it was another guy or something."

Michael glares at her. "What's more, I also heard her say the word 'puffy'." He waits for a reaction but receives none from either Oscar or Jenna. "So, I ask her directly: did you say the words vagina and puffy to your mother? And she says, yes. She's all casual and like, why is this a big deal?"

"Which is a completely reasonable way to respond," says Jenna.

Oscar helplessly shrugs.

"And I'm like, but you're naked. You're talking to your mother about your vagina. Why is that a thing you do?" Michael pauses. "She just shrugs. So I ask, what was it about puffy? And this, *this*, she looks a little embarrassed about, but finally she says, I guess my vagina was a little puffy and I was asking my mom about it. Of course, that freaks me out, because then I'm wondering is this something I did? Was it puffy last night? How did I not notice that? What kind of shit boyfriend am I?"

"You might be a shit boyfriend, but that's probably not the reason," says Jenna.

"Oh, laugh. Sure, laugh at me!" says Michael. He sighs. "I ask her why she's never shared the state of her vagina with me? And she says, because I never asked. Never asked! Wouldn't you think I'd want to know that kind of thing?" Michael looks directly at Oscar.

"I guess?" Oscar says. "I mean, sure. You'd want to know. Right?"

"Right!" says Michael. "I realized I may have gone a little too far, but I couldn't help myself. I was watching the proverbial car tumbling down the side of the cliff, but I was powerless to stop it. This conversation could not end positively, yet I couldn't throw on the brakes. The words just kept falling out of my mouth. That little filter in my head was broken. Completely broken. No hope. No hope now."

Jenna laughs.

"What?" Michael asks.

"I mean, I guess you've grown because at least you realize you're going off the tracks. That's growth, I guess."

Michael shakes his head. "She says that she's always had that kind of conversation with her mom and probably always will."

"Seems healthy to me," says Oscar. "I mean, I think society has built up a lot of unnecessary walls and boundaries around what's polite to talk about.

Jenna nods.

"But that means she's talking to her mom about our sex life, and that involves me," says Michael. "I mean. Awkward. Right?"

"Or," Jenna gestures to Oscar as if his words still hung in the air, "Healthy. You know, take your pick."

Michael sighs. "You guys, I swear. But get this. Then, and this is the thing that really did it, she says: this conversation is making me uncomfortable." Michael's hands gesture wildly and waits for a reaction. None comes. "Jesus. Seriously, you too?"

"Honestly," says Oscar. "This conversation is making me feel a little uncomfortable. So I guess I get it?"

"I wish I could help you here," says Jenna. "But I love that Charlie has that kind of relationship with her mother. It's important for women to be able to talk about their health. And you should also be happy that Charlie thinks enough about you to be talking to her mother about you."

"As the cause of puffiness? An irritation?" asks Michael.

"Even as the cause of an irritation," says Jenna. "Come on, when was the last time you had a serious relationship that lasted this long? And was this healthy? You're just freaking out because you're getting close to something resembling normal and you found someone who tolerates your shit."

"Or, maybe tolerated?" asks Michael.

"Past tense?" Oscar asks. "Oof. Sorry, man."

"Well, our conversation didn't go well after that," says Michael. "I guess I overreact sometimes."

"Sometimes?" asks Jenna.

Michael nods. "But how can I look her mother in the eye now? Knowing that she's been part of this conversation?"

"The same way she'll look at you, knowing you're in a relationship with her daughter?" asks Oscar.

"Zing!" says Jenna. "Nice one, Oscar."

"Man," says Michael. He finally stops his pacing. "How do I manage to continually fuck this up? Over and over again?"

"The good news is, it seems like you found someone who appreciates you're trying and understands that you're not going to get it right all the time," says Jenna. "Just go talk to her."

"And maybe take some flowers," says Oscar. "I know they're cliché and they don't necessarily fix anything themselves, but most women like them."

"Plus, if nothing else," says Jenna. "She'll have to stop to find a vase to put them in, and that will give you a little time to talk before she throws you out."

Michael glares at Jenna.

"I'm just kidding," says Jenna. "You'll be fine. Don't overthink it. Just go talk to her."

"Now?" asks Michael.

"Now," Jenna and Oscar say at the same time.

"Okay, thanks," says Michael. He shows himself out

and closes the door behind him.

"Where were we?" asks Jenna.

"I was apologizing about the Beatles."

"And I was saying they're doing just fine, they don't need your apology."

"Right."

"Good," says Jenna.

"And now?" asks Oscar.

"Ever wonder why dogs got a position named after them? Why not turtles?"

"Well, I think turtle-style is perhaps a little more difficult to describe. Plus, dogs are a more common animal," says Oscar.

Jenna laughs, "Look at you, always the practical one."

TRIPLE DATE COFFEE

Oscar and Jenna are sitting at a table on the third floor of Tree Town, speaking quietly. Time has passed again, but just how many days or weeks or months is difficult to discern from the clues provided. Sunny Hodge's cover of AC/DC's "Hells Bells" is playing in the background. Charlie and Michael approach the table, and Jenna and Oscar stand. They share hugs and handshakes, and then sit down at the table again. A moment later, Louise and Kathy arrive as well. The same standing/hugging/handshaking routine is repeated.

Kathy gestures at Michael. "So, I see you have indeed become an adult."

"I like to think we've both grown a little," says Charlie, smiling at Kathy and then at Michael.

"Uh huh, what she said," Michael says, giving Kathy a dirty look and then smiling.

"So," Jenna starts. "Michael and Charlie, this is Oscar. Oscar, this is Michael and Charlie. And of course, you already know Louise and Kathy."

Polite smiles and nods are exchanged.

"Jenna says you're studying mass communication?"

asks Michael.

"Yeah," says Oscar. "It seemed like a logical way to go. You know, I mean when do you not want to communicate with the masses? It seemed like it would work for any job I might apply for later."

The others half-heartedly nod.

"Do they put something special in the coffee here?" asks Charlie. "I think this could be addictive."

"That might explain why this is like a second home for Kathy, Jenna, and Michael," Louise says.

"They do spend a lot of time here," says Charlie. "But, you know, this place does have a certain kind of charm to it. The music, the tree, the view of State Street."

An awkward silence ensues.

Oscar laughs to break the tension. "The last time we were together," Oscar makes a circle around Kathy, Louise, and Jenna, and concludes with himself, "you all ganged up on me. Promise to play nice this time?"

Kathy laughs.

"Oh, I had your back," says Louise, but she nods.

"I did apologize," says Jenna.

"I know, I know," says Oscar, laughing.

Another awkward silence ensues.

"Oh!" says Charlie. "Funny story for you."

The others are relieved from the awkwardness and lean in.

"The other day," Charlie continues. "I was at the gym. My apartment complex has a gym. It's not huge, but it has two ellipticals, two treadmills, two bikes, and a few free weights."

Charlie walks into the gym. Two TVs hang from ceiling mounts. Each is aimed towards one half of the room. Aside from the exercise equipment, there is little else in the way of decoration. There is one other woman (29) jogging on the treadmill. The TV is on quite loud, the closed captioning is on, and the woman is wearing headphones.

Charlie eyes the woman who doesn't notice her. Charlie begins to jog on the treadmill and turns the TV on that faces her half of the room. After channel surfing, she settles on the news. The volume from the other TV is loud enough that Charlie adjusts the volume of hers to twenty-five, and still can't really hear her program. Finally, she enables the closed captioning and settles into her run.

The woman stops running and begins to use a Pilates ball. After a few sit-ups, she stops to let a man (32) into the gym. The man begins doing curls with small dumbbells towards the back of the gym. The woman leaves the Pilates ball out and begins to run on the treadmill again.

As Charlie runs, the volume from the other TV increases dramatically, to the point where Charlie's program cannot be heard. Charlie eyes the woman and then adjusts her own TV until it's at thirty-two. The volume of the woman's TV increases again. Charlie adjusts hers until it is at the same level as the woman's.

Suddenly, Charlie's TV turns off. Charlie turns it back on. Almost immediately, it turns off again. The woman is holding a universal control and glaring at Charlie.

"How fucking rude," the woman says, still running. "We were here first. You don't have to turn that shit up so loud. Who listens to the news when they run anyway?"

Charlie stares at the woman dumbfoundedly. Both because she's hardly winded, but also at the nerve. "Uhm, I only turned it up because I couldn't hear the TV over your program. And, I might add, you are wearing headphones. So I really don't understand why you needed the TV to be so loud, or to have any sound at all."

"Right! To block out idiots like you," the woman says.

The woman makes a scoffing sound and looks over her shoulder at the man lifting weights. He does not notice.

"Can you believe that?" Charlie asks. "It was insane."

"Wow," says Jenna. "I really don't know what to say. Wow."

"Did you finish your jog?" asks Michael.

"Yeah," says Charlie. She shrugs. "Of course. I probably burned more calories because I was so angry."

"People like that just make it difficult to have any faith in humanity," says Louise.

Conrad arrives and refills mugs.

"I can understand," says Oscar.

Conrad, Jenna, Michael, Louise, Kathy, and Charlie all look at Oscar, clearly astonished.

"I listen to my iPod and watch TV," says Oscar. "I like the combination of noises. I tune one in and the other out, depending on what catches my ear."

"But, you wouldn't get in a fight like that, would you?" asks Jenna.

The other observers' heads move like someone watching tennis, bouncing from Oscar to Jenna and back as the conversation volleys back and forth.

"I guess it depends," says Oscar.

"On?" asks Jenna.

"Well, I have my routine," says Oscar. "I don't like people messing with it. I mean, it's a public space, right?"

Charlie realizes this is a question for her. "Oh, technically, it's a shared private space, but I think I get what you mean."

"Right," says Oscar. "You need a card to get in. Sure, but for people who live there, it's a shared space. Everyone has to get along. The first person in sets the tone for the rest of the people."

"So, by virtue of being there 'first', you get to determine the volume of the TV, the temperature, and everything else in the room?" asks Jenna.

"Well, of course you could ask to adjust or change things," says Oscar.

"Uh huh," says Jenna. "But the first person there is King of the Gym? And his peons can apply for permission to adjust the volume?"

"That sounds a bit harsh," says Oscar. "But essentially. Yes."

"Wow," says Conrad. "Those are some balls you got there, kid. We have a wheelbarrow if you need some help on the way out."

Oscar eyes Conrad. "I feel like I'm being made into the bad guy and I wasn't even there and haven't done anything. All I'm saying is, as the second person in the room, if you want to change something, ask. Communication is important and I think we just assume things about one another and then are outraged when someone doesn't see it the same way."

"I don't think you'll get any argument from us that communication is important," says Charlie. "And, I should asked or said something. I was behaving just as childishly as she was."

Oscar shrugs and nods.

Conrad walks towards the stairs shaking his head.

The group sits in awkward silence again.

Michael breaks that silence. "So much for a funny story, eh? I know, let's talk about sex or politics or religion. Those are safe topics, right?"

Charlie elbows Michael.

"Well, we can't really stay long anyway," says Kathy.

She and Louise put their mugs down at the same time.

"Big news coming soon," says Louise.

"Hush!" says Kathy. "God, you're so bad at keeping secrets!"

"You can't tell us about a secret and then not tell us what it is," says Jenna. "Not fair."

"It's not a secret," says Kathy. "It's a surprise. Secrets you don't share, surprises you do. The reveal is just delayed. Which is the case here."

"Soon!" says Louise.

"Soon," echoes Michael.

DROWNING SORROWS

This is definitely a time-passing chapter. Think of it as little vignettes of moments with our characters in different settings as the leaves change color, the holidays come and go, and the snow begins to fly and the calendar flips through the remaining months of 2011.

Jenna sits at her laptop reading emails from customers. One email in particular catches her eye. She reads and re-reads it.

Dear Love Formula creators,

I know most people probably shoot for the stars when they're looking for matches. But, my husband and I used your service when it first came out and we are so happy. According to your formula, we were only a 75% match. But either your formula is faulty or there's a lot of wiggle room in the final 25%, because neither of us can imagine wanting anything more out of a partner. So, we write to say: thanks for helping us find our match! And to suggest maybe the formula needs some tweaking. We feel like we're 100% here.

Warmly, Cassandra and Jim

Jenna closes her laptop and flops her head against her couch cushion. She sighs, stares at the ceiling, and then closes her eyes. Blindly, she gropes for her cell phone which is sitting on the coffee table. Eyes still closed, she speed-dials Oscar.

Charlie and Michael are sitting on Charlie's couch.

"So," says Charlie. "Bugs?"

"Bugs," Michael confirms. "Look, I understand if you're wigged out. But that's what that was all about." He looks at Charlie, carefully examining her for a reaction.

"What? Do I have a booger hanging from my nose?" she asks.

"No, but you don't look as horrified as I thought you might."

"Well. The sheet thing. That's my quirk. I hate clothes. They feel so claustrophobic. Same with sheets. When I get home after a day of dealing with being held in, I just need a break. So, expect nudity."

"I can accept that." He winks and smiles. "As long as you're cool with me wearing undies to bed."

"Or maybe we could buy you a small, personal-size blanket?"

Michael leans over to Charlie and kisses her. They embrace. His cell phone buzzes on the coffee table. It's Jenna.

Kathy and Louise are walking hand-in-hand across the University of Michigan diag. When they reach the mid-point, at the giant M, they stop. Kathy takes a knee, looks up at Louise, and produces a small box from her pocket. She opens the box, presents the ring to Louise, and slips it on her left finger. Louise smiles, cries, and pulls Kathy to her feet and holds her. Kathy's cell phone pokes out of her purse and is vibrating. Jenna is calling. The call goes unanswered.

Conrad is wiping down the counter with a towel and whistling while he works. The bell over the door jingles as Jenna enters. She storms towards the counter. Operation Ivy's "Bankshot" is playing.

"Barista? Baristo?" she considers the words. "Give me a shot."

Conrad pulls out an espresso cup and begins to make the drink. He eyes her curiously.

"On second thought," she says. "Make it a double."

Conrad raises his eyebrow but resumes his work. "So, what's up? Where's the rest of the gang?" He slides the espresso shot to Jenna.

"No idea," she says. "They're doing something more important than answering my calls. Which is fine, good for them. I'm happy."

"You don't sound happy."

"Well, happy for them, anyway," she says.

"Something on your mind?" Conrad asks.

"What's with the music?" Jenna asks.

"I can tell you're changing the subject," Conrad says, "but I'll allow it. When it's slow, I play whatever I want."

"You mean you typically play what your patrons want?" she asks.

"Not exactly," Conrad says. "But, how about this, during regular hours, when we're busier, I give more thought to what's being played than I do when it's slow."

Jenna nods.

"I mean, it's all music I enjoy. This I just enjoy more and assume most people might not."

Jenna pounds the shot and then winces.

"Another, give me another. Another double," she says.

"Yes ma'am."

The song fades out and Fishbone's "Swim" begins playing.

Conrad works on another espresso and Jenna glances at her cell phone. No notifications.

"Conrad," Jenna says. "Dearest, oldest friend. Conrad."

"Is that a crack about my age?"

Jenna scowls at him. He puts up his hands and slides the shot towards her.

"All I'm saying," Conrad says. "Is, while I appreciate the sentiment, I'm not sure frequenting my establishment for the last decade really constitutes as a friendship."

"Oh, I'm more than just a frequenter of your establishment."

"Sure," says Conrad. "But what do you really know about me? Or what do I really know about you?"

"I know about your tattoos and that you like Funguys."

"Fugazi," Conrad corrects her.

"Whatever," says Jenna. "I know about you and Grover and that you've turned over a new leaf. And that you used to run that record company."

"I'm not suggesting you don't know things about me," says Conrad. "Or even more about me than some people know. I just think that friends go much deeper than that."

"Shut up," says Jenna. "Just play along."

"Fair enough. Okay, what's up, bestie?" Conrad rests his hands on his chin and bats his eyelashes, but Jenna isn't looking and doesn't notice.

"I need some advice." She charges on.

"Well, for starters, I suggest you slow down. Isn't that burning the roof of your mouth? Plus, you're going to be up all night."

Jenna ignores his interjection and continues, "About

guys. Guys, Conrad. And while I talk, give me another. Double."

"Uh huh," says Conrad. "You come to me, the guy who has all the answers about relationships. Because I'm known for my stable girlfriends. What with dating younger women who work for me. Yeah, that worked out really well. I am the obvious choice, the sage upon the hill."

Jenna sighs and shrugs. "I don't know what to do. Plus, you turned that around. Right?"

Conrad slides her the shot. "Look, you're smart. You'll figure it out. You have that formula thing, your good looks, your youth, and you have at least two qualified guys waiting on you. Though, that Oscar kid is… I don't know. Anyway, no one can tell you the right answer here. Let your heart and brain duke it out. They usually come up with a decent compromise. It's when you let one rule over the other that problems ensue."

Jenna nods and slams the shot. "Hey, thanks. I really do appreciate it."

"Christ, I should set up a jar like Lucy from *Peanuts* did and charge at least a quarter for this quality advice. It's shit you already know, you just need a clear head to see it."

"Another double."

"Are you kidding me?" He fills a glass with water and slides it to her. "I don't want you going anywhere until you've had at least four of these. Sit over there and think. It's what the doctor ordered."

"But—"

"No. Take it and go. I'm watching you."

Jenna takes the glass of water and sits down at an empty table on the first floor. She sips the water and watches people pass by on the street outside.

Days have passed since the late night at Tree Town,

Jenna is walking the streets of Ann Arbor wearing a thick sweater and jeans. In a film, you'd recognize some of the buildings she passes by as being near Oscar's apartment. She's circling and circling and clearly avoiding stopping at his place. Everything in the windows appears interesting.

She looks at some sneakers and thinks, *oh wow those shoes are fabulous*. But, in truth, they're just Vans and nothing special.

Never heard of that book title before, but she stops to peruse them as if she doesn't have a huge stack of books waiting to be read at home.

Those clothes, oh wow, really wonderful. It's basically the same outfit she's wearing now.

Finally, Jenna zeroes in on Oscar's apartment. Unlike hers, it doesn't have a buzzer. There's no pretense of security. She walks the halls until she finds his door and knocks.

"Oh hey," Oscar says. "Haven't seen you in a while."

She nods.

"What's going on?" he asks. "Sorry, I've been busy with classes and studying. I know I haven't been the best boyfriend in the world." He pauses. "Want to come in?"

"No," she says. "And that's fine. I think…" she trails off and doesn't finish her thought.

"Oh no," Oscar says.

"I think," she tries again and pauses trying to find the right word, "I think we're maybe not as 100% as I thought we were."

"It depends how you measure it," Oscar says.

"What do you mean?"

"Well, I mean, it depends on the scoring variables and what you measure," Oscar says. "If shared musical taste is ranked highly."

Jenna interrupts, "it's not just that."

"Or maybe urination habits are scored heavily."

"Or that," Jenna says.

"I just mean," Oscar says, "and I guess I don't even know why I'm fighting this when you've already made up your mind, but I'll say it anyway: the system is rigged."

"Why do you say that?" Jenna had not expected that response.

"Come on, you literally wrote the formula," Oscar says. "If you write the test, you're going to do a hell of a lot better on it than anyone who didn't."

"It's not biased though," says Jenna.

"Of course, it's biased," Oscar says. "Everything is. You can't help but cook bias into things like that. Any kind of scale or measure or test or evaluation. There's no such thing as objectivity."

Jenna looks down at her shoes, shaking her head slowly. She says, "I'm sorry."

"Me too," says Oscar. "But it was fun while it lasted."

Jenna nods. "Thank you."

Oscar laughs. "I don't know that I've ever had anyone say, 'thank you' during a breakup, but, you know, I should thank you, too."

"Oh?"

"Only fair right? I mean, you learn things from relationships," Oscar says. "About what works and what doesn't, and you learn about yourself."

Jenna nods and smiles.

"So, thank you, too," Oscar says.

They stand smiling at each other until Jenna breaks the silence.

"Okay, I'm going run," she says. "Probably put on some winter music and brood a bit and try to figure myself out."

"Sounds like a plan," Oscar says. "I have to study for those finals. But I'm sure we'll see each other around."

Jenna waves and walks back down the hall and out of the building.

AN ANNOUNCEMENT

Kathy's apartment is full of people. Charlie and Michael are sitting next to one another in bar stools at the counter in the kitchen. Kathy is busy at the stove and Jenna is hovering over her shoulder trying to figure out what she's cooking. Louise is sipping wine on the couch. Tom Petty's "The Waiting" is playing in the background.

Michael stands up from his bar stool. "Alright, alright. Enough with all this. What's the secret? What's the announcement?"

"You mean, you don't know?" asks Charlie. "God, guys are so unobservant."

"What?" Michael asks. "Help me out here."

Louise holds up her left hand and wiggles it back and forth.

Michael waves back.

Jenna presses the palm of her hand into her forehead. "You don't see anything new? Something that didn't used to be there? Something that might suggest that some major change has occurred?" She pauses, waiting before adding, "Perhaps in status?"

Michael looks at Louise's hand, which is still raised.

Jenna shakes her head. "They're engaged. That's an engagement ring, doofus."

"Oh! Oh! I did notice the ring, I just didn't think, I don't know—" Michael stammers and eventually bursts out with, "Congratulations!"

"Thank you," says Louise. She stands up from the couch. "There is a bit more of an announcement. The original announcement was that we were going on a short vacation to New York. But Kathy just couldn't wait. We weren't supposed to do rings. She proposed yesterday."

"I couldn't help myself," says Kathy.

"Of course, I noticed you're wearing a matching ring," says Jenna. "I guess you were feeling left out?"

Kathy looks at Jenna and smiles. "Something like that."

"So, when are you going? For how long? Are we invited?" asks Charlie. "All those important questions that Michael probably won't think to ask."

"Hey! I was getting to that," says Michael. He looks at Louise and Kathy, who are sitting together on the couch now, holding hands. "When are you going? How long? Are we invited?" he says. He looks at Charlie. "Anything else?"

Charlie holds her head and shakes it slowly, letting out a small sigh as she does so.

"We just bought the tickets," says Louise. "We leave in two weeks. We'll only be gone for five days."

"Wow, that's fast," says Michael.

Charlie frowns at him.

"I mean, short engagement?" Michael attempts.

Charlie sighs again.

"Frankly," says Kathy, "we weren't really sure marriage was an option for a while there. We kept following the different laws, and it didn't help that Michigan passed legislation making same-sex marriage illegal a few years ago."

Louise groans. "It certainly doesn't make this feel like home."

"Much less HOMES," says Michael, laughing at his joke. "What? You know, the pneumonic for remembering the Great Lakes?"

"Read the room, man," Jenna says.

"Sorry," Michael says and mimes zipping his lips shut.

"As I was saying," Kathy continues, "we've known for a while, but just didn't know what to do about it. For instance, did I want to be part of the patriarchal system that rejects me?"

"Or did I," Louise adds, "feel the need to formalize our love with a document certified by a state?"

"All good questions," Jenna says, nodding. "But clearly, you decided you did, right?"

Kathy and Louise laugh.

"Well, not at all that," Kathy says. "But ultimately, we wanted it more than we didn't. Is that fair?" She looks at Louise.

"Completely," Louise says. "So, as Michael pointed out, yes, it's a short engagement. But the engagement period is really ambiguous anyway."

"As Beyonce says, I liked it so," Kathy trails off.

Louise laughs and blushes.

"When you know, you just know," Kathy says, "So, since New York passed their Marriage Equality Act, we're headed to NYC!"

"Are you doing a honeymoon?" asks Jenna.

"This is kind of an all-in-one package," says Louise. "I don't really have a lot of time off, so we'll land, get married, and then spend the rest of time enjoying ourselves in the city."

"I've never been," says Kathy.

"And I haven't been there since before 2001," says

Louise. "Will be interesting to see how the city has changed."

Everyone nods.

"But we'll be there long enough to have a little fun though," says Kathy. "It isn't that we didn't want to invite you, but it's short notice and we just want some time alone."

"I'm so happy for you both," Jenna says. "Too bad your home state isn't up with the times yet to allow you to get married here, but you'll have fun and that's all that really matters."

Kathy shrugs. "They'll get there. Plus, this way, it's an excuse to see *The Book of Mormon* musical we keep hearing about." Kathy gets up from the couch, gives Jenna a hug, and checks on dinner.

"I heard that show is hilarious," Michael says, breaking his silence.

"Hard to believe those gross-out guys from South Park have done something more highbrow," says Charlie. She laughs. "But I've heard some of the jokes and songs are— just wow."

"We should plan a trip," Michael says, turning to Charlie.

She smiles. "That would be fun."

"Okay," Kathy says, "it looks like dinner is ready."

RECIPES FOR RUTABAGAS

Jenna is asleep in her bed. The sun streams through the window and the alarm clock reads: 11:11 a.m. Her cell phone rings on the side table. She rolls over, reaches for it, and manages to knock it on the floor. It continues to ring three more times. When she finally holds the phone, she receives a text message from Kathy: *we did it!*

Jenna smiles at the phone as if Kathy is able to see it, and then sends a reply: *I'm so happy for you.* Then she closes her eyes again.

The alarm clock now reads 4:52 p.m. It's obvious Jenna hasn't left her bed all day. She stirs, scratches her head, and gets up. After digging through various clothing options, she opts for a pair of gray sweatpants, a white tank top, and a dark blue hoodie. She pulls her hair into a ponytail and heads for the door.

The radio in Jenna's car plays Def Leppard's "Too Late for Love" as she navigates the streets. She changes the channel and The Breeder's "It's the Love" plays for a couple of beats until she changes the channel a last time and finds The Cure's "The Lovecats." She smiles, pulls into a parking space at Whole Foods, turns off the engine, and walks inside.

Jenna pushes a shopping cart through the aisles. She is lost in thought as she meanders through the store haphazardly throwing items into her cart. The store's speaker system plays Styx's "Too Much Time on My Hands." She stops at various produce, pondering and considering. She holds a rutabaga in her hand and looks at its various spirals of white and purple. A voice draws her out of her daze.

"Rutabaga. Bold choice. I've been trying to eat local. You know?" He pauses. "Well, as local as Whole Foods gets anyway."

Jenna turns to the voice and stares at David.

"The thing is," says David, "as winter sets in on Michigan, eating local is harder and harder to do. I'd miss the citrus. And, as much as I'd love to subsist on root vegetables and whatnot available here seasonally… I just don't know many ways to prepare rutabaga."

"My grandmother used to make pasties. She always used rutabagas in them."

"What's a pastie?" asks David. "Aren't those the things that, you know?" He stammers. "Tassels? That dancers wear?"

Jenna still isn't getting it.

He groans. "Tassels that dancers put on their nipples?" He mimes the motion with twirling fingers over his nipples.

"What?" asks Jenna, shocked. "Uhm, no. Two very different things. However, now you have forever burned the image of my grandmother with, ugh, spinning tassels."

David laughs.

"Sure, laugh it up. It's not seared into your brain."

David laughs harder.

"No. Just no. I mean, *pah-sties*, not *pay-sties*, which are kind of like a pot pie. The miners used to eat them. They have a thick crust so they could hold onto them, and eat the inside," Jenna pauses. "Wait a minute, I thought you were mad at me."

"Mad?" asks David. "About what?"

"About, you know, the whole one hundred percent thing," says Jenna.

David shrugs. "A guy can't change his mind? Besides, we're just talking. In a grocery store. About recipes. Right?"

Jenna considers this and smiles.

"Plus, truly and honestly," David says. "I was never mad at you."

"Just disappointed?" asks Jenna.

"No." David shakes his head. "That sounds terrible, like something a parent would say to their child. I wasn't disappointed, I was just sad. Mostly because I knew, you know, like *knew*. And clearly, you didn't. It's hard when there's a difference of opinion. I mean, what are you going to do, force someone to be with you? That's hardly humane or reasonable or a foundation for a lasting relationship."

Jenna nods slowly. She's not sure how to respond, so she continues the earlier theme of recipes, "You can also use rutabaga in soups. I know a few recipes for those. Plus, you can mash them like potatoes, or roast them like other vegetables, or treat them like turnips. Put them in stew."

"Well, who knew you were a walking rutabaga cookbook?" David smiles.

"Yeah, I guess we should include something like that on our dating profile, huh?" She smiles apologetically at David. "I'm sorry. I really am."

David smiles and looks at her shopping cart. There's an odd assortment of things in her cart—mostly impulse buys. "Interesting mix." He gestures at the cart.

"Yeah," she says with a shrug.

"Shopping without a list? That seems very unlike you. You probably have a hundred dollars worth of groceries here, and I really don't know that any of those combine to make a single meal," David says.

Jenna looks at her hodge-podge of groceries and frowns. "Maybe I've changed a bit? I mean, a girl can change, right?" She pauses before adding, "I really am sorry."

David smiles and grabs two medium size rutabagas. He weighs the rutabagas in his hands and puts both into his cart.

"I don't know what else to say," Jenna says. "Thanks for—"

David waves his hands in the air and whispers, "shhhhh." He looks around conspiratorially. "I got the rutas, you got the recipes. Feel like coming over and showing me how to use these things? Plus, I think you'll like some of the vinyl I bought the other day. What do you say?"

Jenna smiles. They walk towards the front of the store talking as The Darkness' "I Believe in a Thing Called Love" plays over the store speakers.

NO NET

Romantic comedies often end with a wedding. Usually, it's between the two main characters, but occasionally it's only set up to look like the couple will get married and then it's slowly revealed that our lovers are only attending a wedding. It's implied that theirs will come—perhaps with a little more growth and time and opportunity to heal from the travails of what has occurred in the previous ninety (or so) minutes, because romantic comedies are rarely much over the one and a half hour mark in duration.

Other times, one of the characters will need to race— on a bike, in a car, by foot—to catch the other before he or she makes some life-altering, door-closing, decision. Perhaps it's heading to the airport or going to give their hand to another in marriage or join a convent. (I'm honestly not sure "going to a convent" has ever been a threat in a romantic comedy, but it sounded funny.)

If not a wedding or a chase to profess their love, then sometimes it's a flashforward, or a montage of "what happens next" (sometimes with short clips that turn to still photographs and capture smiling faces or freeze on a funny moment.)

Maybe it ends with a tender moment as the music swells and you can see—but cannot hear—whispered dialogue.

It could always be one character making a grand romantic gesture. A public proclamation of love. Forgoing a promotion or dream job to remain in the same city as their love.

Maybe they just walk into the fog together, holding hands.

In this one, we end with a party.

Imagine the song "Pieces of the People We Love," by The Rapture, playing. Snow falls outside the window and accumulates on the several inches already obscuring the sidewalks and streets. The TV is tuned to the local news. As we focus on the TV, the music quiets but never quite completely mutes.

The announcer reports: "Thanks for the sports update, Tim. Always good to hear about those Tigers, particularly when they're on a winning streak. In other news, the co-creator of The Love Formula has found love using her own formula. When asked the percentage of her match, she stated, 'First, that information is confidential. But second, and I think most of our users know this, love isn't just a numbers game.' Let's take a look—"

The TV turns off. David holds the remote.

"Heck of a day they picked for a reception," says Jenna.

"I'm sure they were more concerned about the event than the possibility of snow," says David.

Jenna ties a scarf around her neck. "Yeah, yeah. You ready?"

David zips his coat and nods. The pair leaves the apartment and the song's volume increases again, muffling any conversation they might have along the way.

David and Jenna walk through the snow, kicking

trenches through it. They hold hands as they walk. They approach Tree Town Coffee and see a sign on the front door that reads: "Closed for Private Party." David opens the door and holds it for Jenna as she walks in.

Tree Town is decorated to celebrate the marriage of Kathy and Louise. Tables are set up in the normally large open space, each table features different foods. There is a sign on the front counter that reads: "Mugs here, coffee there, help yourself." None of the usual workers are present.

Kathy and Louise are talking in a small group of people. Other voices can be heard coming from the levels above. Charlie's laugh can clearly be heard. David and Jenna approach the group. Cosmo is the first to notice their approach, he smiles and waves, drawing attention to their arrival.

Conrad appears from a back room with Grover; they are holding hands and smiling.

Jenna raises her eyebrows at him and Conrad holds up his finger with the mustache tattoo in response. Jenna laughs. David and Jenna join the circle of friends where Kathy and Louise are and greet them with hugs. Michael says something and the whole group laughs.

The beat of the song continues even as the image fades into the credits.

What's next?

Maybe outtakes? Or a blooper reel? Perhaps Polaroids of scenes from favorite moments, or a glimpse into the future? Is there going to be a mid-credit, or end-credit scene? Maybe one of the characters will break the fourth wall and speak directly to the camera asking, "You're still here? It's over. Go home. Go."

No, not for this story. This one ends here with a happy moment. These moments—where an entire group of friends are all happy and content—are rare and hard to come by, so let's just let the characters enjoy it while it lasts. Surely, they'll have future challenges and arguments and disagreements and struggles, but for now, I'm going to leave it right there.

ABOUT THE AUTHOR

Originally from Michigan, Michael MacBride now calls Minnesota home. He has delivered newspapers, worked for UPS, delivered pizzas, done collections at a bank, was a roadie for a country band, was a grant-writer and funder-researcher for non-profits, taught English, Literature, and Humanities courses at universities and colleges in Minnesota, New Hampshire, Ohio, and Illinois, and held a few other jobs in between.

And yes, he absolutely loves a good romcom. In particular, *Stranger Than Fiction*, *Love Actually*, and *The Princess Bride*.